SANTILMO

From the jungle it comes...
The vengeful spirit

Arthur Crandon

Arthur Crandon Publishing

*2020 has been a strange year. A house move,
2 books published, and a pandemic, which
I have managed to avoid. My writing is ably
supported by my wife, Lynnie Requime Ceniza,
and is hindered by my wonderful three year
old son, Cameron. Despite everything, life is
good, thanks to these two wonderful people.*

CONTENTS

FOREWORD

The mysterious tropical islands of the Philippines hold many secrets. Many distant parts of the country are, as yet, unexplored.

The people are kind and loving, but with an uncanny belief in the supernatural. Stories of mythical creatures of all sorts abound and are largely believed.

Pixies (Dwende), Vampires (Aswang), Giants, fairies, witches, ogres and other nightmare provoking monsters abound.

The Santilmo is one such beast. It is murderous and frightening - but it is not all bad...

CHAPTER 1.

UNREST IN THE VILLAGE

In the still soft ground at the side of the dirt track, a fat rat gnaws on a pili nut cast down earlier by the violent storm. The air is fresh following the monsoon of the night before, and the skies are clear.

Slowly, the waking forest finds its voice with the early morning cackling of the small black maya birds as they flit between coconut and mango trees. The birds have been busy for hours already, feasting on the bugs, thick in the air, thrown up by the storm. A lone monkey shrieks and sends them scattering as he moves from branch to branch, disturbing the rat and sending it scurrying back into the bushes, the nut still in its mouth.

Mabuhay is a small village in Southern Philippines, about ten miles from the nearest town, Maranding. The settlement comprises just twenty huts, each housing a large family and built around a communal square. The dwellings are rudely built from bamboo, with roofs made from Anihaw leaves that need to be replaced after severe storms.

Ophelia skips along, scuffing her well-worn shoes against the still muddy ground. It is only six a.m. as she emerges from her hut; she had risen early. She bathed, singing quietly to herself before her family awoke. It is her eighteenth birthday and she will make the most of it. Her mum has bought some meat – they will eat roast pig tonight. This is a rare treat.

She is unusually keen to fetch water for her mother today. The stooped old lady smiles and thanks her, knowing she just wants to show off her dress. Her mother is filled with pride as she watches her only daughter skip gaily along the dirt road.

At five feet six inches Ophelia is tall for a Philippina, but slim and elegant as are most of the village girls.

The village has a hand-drawn well, with good water. Nearby villages share the source, which seldom runs dry.

Around her the villagers are waking up and the sounds and smell of the forest begin to fill the streets; older women walk past her carrying baskets of washing, on their path down to the river.

A group of men, hoes slung over their shoulders, nod to her on their way to the fields. She smiles at everybody, hoping someone will notice her neat dress; her only smart dress. It's yellow, but faded, sleeveless and with white edging ending modestly just above the knee. Her father bought it two years ago. It barely fits her now, but her mother says she's stopped growing so she doesn't need another one. It comes out for special occasions: Christmas, Easter, Fiesta and, of course, Birthdays.

A tall young man stops to chat with her.

Sam is the only one to return her smile. The good-looking youth is just a few years older than Ophelia, and a fisherman, like his father. Shirtless, like all the other village lads, he wears faded blue jeans cut off just below the knee. He is bare-footed, as are all the other youths; they have no need for shoes.

'Good morning, Phe. You look nice today.' He regrets saying it as soon as the words leave his mouth, but she is sharp, and pounces.

'Don't I look good other times?' she tries to appear upset, but fails, and laughs.

Ophelia doesn't really take offence; she just wants to tease him. The discussion gives her an excuse to join him and walk by his side down the street. Her birthday could not have got off to a better start.

'Are you going fishing today?' She needs to keep the conversation going.

'I will later. I must help my dad. There's been some storm damage to the house after the rains. I have to assist him with that first.' he responds.

'We're lucky, our house is ok. If you have time, come round later. Mum's cooking tonight.'
Sam's eyes light up. He will make time. He's held a torch for the pretty girl since she started to become a woman.

'Ok. See you later, I hope your day goes well.'

She smiles and watches him disappear down the street, her eyes resting on him until he turns the corner. Her father says she is still too young for courting, but she plans to ask him again later today, she is eighteen now after all.

Ophelia is one of the luckier girls. Her father,

Celmar, is a fisherman and the village captain. Unlike some, her family rarely goes hungry. She excels at the school in nearby Maranding town her parents send her to, but now she wants to go to university in Manila to study law. She hasn't told her father yet. Although better off than most families in the village, they are not really well off. Perhaps her dad can't afford to send her. She will wait for the right moment to ask.

As she pumps the fresh water into her bucket, she sees a horse and cart in the distance, but getting closer. The bucket spills as she puts it down and runs towards the oncoming wagon which pulls up as she approaches. A smiling grey-haired man jumps down just in time to accept her embrace.

'Hi daddy, we didn't expect you until lunch time, I'm glad you're early.'

'I'm pleased to be home too sweetheart, but I've got disturbing news, that is why I left the town early, to get back and tell everybody.'

Ophelia's smile dies on hearing her father's words.

'What is it, father?' Ophelia asks, her brow creasing at his grim tone. 'Whatever is the matter?' All notion of her birthday is gone.

'Maybe it's nothing to worry about, but we need to consider the situation and prepare. Run along ahead of me and gather the elders at the house. Tell your mother to get ready for a meeting.

Ophelia runs off towards their home while her father climbs back up on the wagon, wincing as he stretches his damaged calf. Celmar owns the biggest boat in the village. But, since a wild pig gored his leg on a hunt a few years ago, he walks with a limp and rarely goes out to sea. He lets others use his boat and shares their catch.

As village Captain, Celmar visits Maranding about once a month to catch up with friends and hear the latest news.

Some houses in the town have electricity, but not all, and one of his richer friends, Elmer, has a radio set – it is the only one for many miles. They always meet at Elmers's house. Two of his sons are working abroad and sending money home. He is building a brick house, two stories, with plastered walls. There are only three such buildings in the town, and Elmers is the only one with a large parlour at the front of the house. These meetings are the only time that Celmar ever feels carpet beneath his feet. Yesterday, Celmar attended a regular meeting at the house. Afterwards, they'd listened to the news from Manila and discussed the situation well into the night.

Until yesterday everyone assumed the war in Europe didn't concern them, they paid scant attention to its progress, but as they gathered around the large brown bakelite radio set. The men heard that Japanese planes and ships have attacked the American fleet in their home port of Pearl Harbour. Thousands have died. Japanese planes and submarines have wiped out the Pacific Fleet, sinking all the ships in port.

Celmar travels home early the next morning as quickly as he can. This news will not wait. As he arrives home, his wife, Maria, brings him coffee. He sits quietly, resting his aching leg and reflecting, while townsfolk gather round and wait for him to speak.

He stands; the gravity of the message demands it. Calmly, he relays the reported events to the hushed meeting. Although there had been rumours, no-one expected this.They receive the news in stunned silence. Ophelia is the first to speak up.

'This is incredibly sad, father, but America is thousands of miles away. How does this affect us?' Celmar smiles and puts his arm around his daughter.

'Sweetheart, the Japanese have been threatening us with occupation for a while, but the Americans have always protected us. There are many U.S. troops still here, but not enough to repel a full invasion. We think the Japanese have attacked the American ships and planes so they cannot come to our aid when the enemy invades our country. Japanese ships have been gathering close to us for a while now.' Celmar's words are sinking in.

'When do you think they will come, daddy? How much time do you think we have?'

'Who can tell, it could be days, or even weeks or months, or they may not come at all, my dear. We must wait and see. There is little we can do anyhow, but if the Japanese come, we can only hope they don't find our tiny village.'

'What about the American soldiers here, won't they protect us?'

'I'm sure they'll do what they can, sweetheart, but without reinforcements they won't hold out long. The Americans in Maranding are already packing up to leave. Their town base is difficult to defend. They'll operate from the jungle from now on.'

As the meeting closes, those by the door were gaze up into the sky, searching for the source of the deep droning noise. It is getting louder.

CHAPTER 2.

THE INVADERS COME

It is not months, or weeks, or even days.

Ten hours after their attack on the U.S. port, the Japanese troops launch their invasion of the Philippine Islands. Troopships arrive in Manila bay; there is little local resistance. Police and other services are busy dealing with the destruction and injuries caused by the blanket bombing of the city that preceded the invasion; they have no resources to confront the invaders. At the same time, hundreds of planes delivering keen young soldiers by parachute to seize the airports and other defense installations appear on the horizon.

In the village, townsfolk emerge from the meeting into the bright sunlight, the startled group shade their eyes against the burning midday sun looking for the source of the noise. Ophelia can count more than seventeen sleek Japanese warplanes passing low overhead before she loses track of the number. They are headed towards Cebu, the largest city in the southern Philippines. The villagers cannot know that, as the invading troops are arriving near Cebu, bombs are already falling on Manila and other major centers a few hundred miles away. Ophelia looks up at her open-mouthed father.

'What will we do? Daddy, I'm scared. Other nearby women are nodding in support. The captain feels he must comfort them.

'There's no need to panic, we're hundreds of miles from anywhere significant. I think if we keep ourselves to ourselves, they'll probably leave us alone – what would they want with us?'

The murmuring group does not seem persuaded. They turn their heads as a voice comes from the back.

'But it's our country. They're taking our country. Who knows what they'll do to us?'

It is Celmar's wife, Maria, who speaks. Her face is taut and she is shaking. Ophelia holds her arm in support.

'We're not soldiers, we're peaceful civilians. Even if they come this far, they won't harm us, as long as we don't cause trouble. The best thing we can do now is wait and see. It will be many days before they get here. There's no point worrying about it yet.' Celmar's comments do little to reassure the group. He does not believe them himself.

The meeting breaks up and people drift off to their own dwellings or their work.

Over the coming days, the relentless and vicious bombing of the major cities continues. The long-planned attack is efficient and coordinated. Two hundred thousand well-armed troops are positioned just off the coast in large boats, awaiting the signal to commence the land invasion as soon as the bombs have done their work. They will destroy infrastructure, damaging vital buildings and transport routes, and demoralising the populace before the inevitable assault.

On the third day after the planes had flown overhead, Celmar returns to Maranding. The village needs more supplies, and he wants to meet with friends who may know what was happening. In Elmer's front room, the men and a few of their wives are huddled around the radio. The mood is somber. For the first time, the announcers have a more menacing tone and are singing a vastly different tune. Advancing Japanese troops seized the radio station on the second day.

'We urge all Filipinos to welcome their Japanese heroes who've come to liberate the oppressed people from their corrupt leaders'.

The sharp female voice said they will be fair, but deal firmly with any dissent. She urges everyone to stay indoors and not congregate in large crowds, at least until the authorities have 'rooted out all remnants of organized and illegal opposition'.

'We have installed our liberating Government in Manila and will install new governors and authorities in the districts. Do not resist. Join us and help build a new nation.'

At the end of the broadcast they played the Japanese anthem. Elmar turns off the set as wisps of smoke drifts upwards from cigarettes and cigars in the otherwise still room.

One of the younger men speaks up.

'How will we know what's going on now? All we're going to get from now on is that propaganda spouting out – I don't want to hear that.' The others nod.

Dennis, a councilman from a nearby township, suddenly rushes through the open door.

'Things are worse than we thought.' He blurts out. Trying to catch his breath, he continues.

'The enemy has reached Cebu. Our soldiers resisted but were overwhelmed in hours. They killed a few, and the rest escaped up into the hills with a few of the American troops.'

Celmar speaks above the excited chatter.

'Come on, we must keep our heads. At least we have the advantage there – we know the territory, but we must prepare.'

The captain keeps his thoughts to himself. In his experience, the Japanese troops are vicious. Celmar's father was in China when the japanese invaded years ago; he got killed in Shanghai. He was a civilian, not a soldier, but they didn't care. The Japs didn't take prisoners. The murderers butchered thousands of people in Nanjing.

Dennis joins in, still winded from his mad dash to the hut.

'Well, Maranding is a small town, they can't be interested in us?'

Celmar shakes his head.

'The U.S. army's based here, isn't it? There's about fifty troops in the barracks across the road.' He looks up through the window and nods at the austere red brick building opposite.

'They'll do their best, but most of them will end up running into the forests and hiding, you know they will. They can't defend us even if they risk their lives trying.'

It is Elmer's turn to speak.

'Look, we're councilmen and captains – everyone will look to us for help and leadership – what are we going to do and say to them?'

Celmar takes the lead.

'Well. I'm going to tell my people to go up into the mountains if they can, but we know many won't. There'll be problems getting food; the elderly and the young will be difficult to move. We've just got to do what we can to survive, and not upset these men, if they come. We can't beat them. If we resist we will get ourselves and our families killed.'

Celmar hurries back to the village to spread the news. His wife, Maria, is close to tears.

'We're not going and leaving you here alone to face them,' she rages.

'Come into the mountains with us. They'll kill you if you stay here.' pleads Maria.

'My dear, I can't. There are many here who can't go. I can't leave them. And anyway, who is going to feed the animals? I've got to stay here and do what I can. You and Ophelia must go, I'll ask for men to take you to a safer place.' She still cries.

Maria wants him to take her and Ophelia deep into the mountains, but she realises he will not leave the vulnerable older and sick folk on their own and knows she cannot change his mind. She gradually calms down.

A party of about twenty, mainly women and

children, and a few of the younger men gather in the square. Sam is among them. Ophelia smiles with relief when she sees him join the group.

There are five guns in the village, two handguns and three rifles. Celmar insists that the lads in the departing group take the guns with them. Maria cannot believe what he is saying. Wide-eyed she implores him.

'Keep the guns, that's your only protection. They could easily kill you.' He holds her close.

'They can kill us whether or not we have guns. If we don't have any weapons, that may be a reason for them not to kill us. If we are no trouble to them, they may leave us alone'

'Sam, can you come over here for a moment please.' Celmar takes the young man aside while the rest of the group are busy with their preparations.

'Try and sneak back here every couple of days if you can. I won't be able to go out foraging in the jungle much, so if you can bring any food it will help. Take care of them, son, I think there will be dark times ahead.' He hugs the boy briefly, then lets him go.

He watches as the group sets off and wonders if he will ever see his wife and daughter again.

CHAPTER 3.

INCREASING DANGER

Celmar smiles and waves confidently at the departing group. Inside, his heart is breaking. He feels the chances of coming through this assault unscathed are not good. The old man is glad when they have withdrawn into the jungle and he can allow the concern to again take over his features.

He turns to see the group that remained in the village, they huddle together in the village square for imagined protection. There are three old ladies and he knows there are two more bedridden who cannot be outside to see their families off.

A small group of elderly men considered too weak for the journey completes the small assembly. They are a sorry looking band. Celmar addresses them.

'We must make the most of this, folks. As far as possible we will carry on village life as before. I hope this conflict will bypass us and we can soon get back to life as it was before.'

Old heads nodded gently, and the group began to disperse to their huts. Celmar looks up at the skies. All is quiet now and it will soon be dusk. He feeds the animals with a heavy heart. He has not told the rest of the village of the rumours he has heard of advancing enemy troops coming closer.

An hour later, and just over a mile away, Ophelia

and her mum sit in a clearing with the others.

'This look a good place. Shall we set up here?'

Sam's father, Raymond Requilme, who is a village elder, comes over to join them.

'We can't stay here Maria, we're right out in the open. Too easy to find, and too easy to attack. We need to be in a higher position, and in thicker jungle.'

He looks around, considering their options.

'We must be hard to spot, higher up on the top of a hill or ridge, and have lookouts to spot any trouble. Luckily at the time of year the vegetation is green and full, if we're careful it will protect us; they won't be able to see us from the air.'

Maria becomes quiet. She remembers that Raymond Requilme spent twelve years in the army, the Philippine Marine Corps, and he has an award for his work fighting the New People Army rebels, ending his distinguished career as a sergeant. She feels reassured at his words.

Raymond looks to the west beyond the trees. It is just possible to see the top of a narrow ridge.

'That should be a good place.' He points to the hill.

'I know the place. The trees are densely packed with high canopies. We will be hidden. They won't be able to spot us from a helicopter, and there's a small stream in the valley below. We'll be fine for fresh water, and maybe some fish.'

At this news the group brightens up and they resume their trek towards the peak Raymond is showing them. The younger boys lead the way, slashing the thicket with their blades to make it easier for the others. Raymond comes forward to stop them.

'I know what you're trying to do, lads, but we mustn't flatten the plants – it will make a trail that will lead anyone right to us, I'm afraid everyone will just have to struggle through, and try to leave as little damage behind them as they can.'

The boys nod and join the others.

Night falls as they reach the top of the ridge. It seems a suitable spot. The woods are dense, and the thirty-meter-wide plateau provides a convenient campsite. We can post lookouts on either side to watch out for movements in the valleys below. The tall baletes trees have a dense canopy, no one in a helicopter can spot them from the air; it is as good a place as any.

The next morning sees Celmar up at dawn and driving the cart towards Maranding. There is no other way to get news. Memories of the planes flying low overhead in the general direction of Cebu haunt him. How far has the enemy come? If they are in Cebu, they can be here in just a few days. He worries they may target Maranding and Mabuhay. These are small settlements, but they're close to a major road between larger cities, strategically, the enemy will need to secure supply routes for Cebu and further on.

Maranding seems quieter, more subdued than usual, as he enters the dusty streets. On reaching the usual meeting house, he greets his old friend who is sitting outside on the porch.

'Hello Celmar, I didn't expect to see you today, but I can guess why you're here. Come on in and have a coffee.'

As the men chat, three large American army trucks trundle past.

'They'll all be gone by the end of the day, you know. My friends in the camp tell me they've been recalled to the larger bases to consolidate. There are only a couple of areas not in enemy control now. They have to get out quickly, some are heading to the coast to get out on boats.'

'We're on our own then.' observes Celmar.

'I guess we are. What can we do? Maranding is too big, and I've got too many people for us to melt into the forests and hide. We just have to stay here and wait, I guess. These are sad times, Celmar, sad times.'

'I've sent most of our village up into the hills. It seemed the best thing to do.' said Celmar..

'We must hope they will leave us alone. Are we getting any news now? I guess there's nothing on the radio now.'

Elmer shakes his head.

'We have no idea what's happening, friend.

Japanese control all the radio stations now. I've asked the other elders to come around this morning. We have to at least discuss the situation.'

They pause their conversation as a large black American sergeant strides down the street and looms up before them.

'Hi guys. How are you holding up?'

He shakes hands with the smaller men.

'Not too well, sergeant. We're sad to see you guys leave.'

'We don't want to go, but it's orders, we have no choice, but I do have some good news.'

He brings two large bags from behind his back. Smiling, he puts them carefully down on the kitchen table.

Celmar steps forward and peeks inside one. Elmer opens the other bag and takes out the two new military grade walkie talkies that are inside. Celmar takes out the other handsets and puts them on the table. They have four new and expensive walkie talkies. While the two elders admire the sets the sergeant picks one up.

'These are state-of-the-art, boys. The captain said I could give them to you. You will not get any useful news on the radio, so we thought you could at least keep in touch with each other – it may help.'

'Thank you, sergeant. These will help us a lot. It's very kind of you.'

'No problem boys; it's the least we can do. We feel bad about leaving you guys.' The sergeant looks up wistfully.

'We know you guys are going to go through hell once we've gone.'

Nobody speaks, there is nothing that needs to be said. The sergeant pulls himself together and forces a smile.

'I've got to run. The last transport is just about to leave. I hope we'll be back, and I'll see you guys again. Bye for now. He strides off before the others can speak, and before he lets his frustration show.

Celmar and Elmer each pick up one of the heavy sets.

'Well, they'll come in useful.' says Elmer.

'You can take two and I'll keep two. You can give a set to your people in the forest so that you can contact each other.' Elmer nods while he studies the device, working out how to use it.

When he is back in Mabuhay he shows the sets to the few remaining villagers.

'At least we'll be able to keep in touch with the others now, I'll give one to Sam tonight.'

Just over a mile away on the ridge, the villagers are settling in. The stream is just a short walk away in the valley; they can hear the gentle trickling from their encampment. The water is fresh and sweet, and the stream opens up into a larger pool a little further on. Small milkfish swim freely and are easy to catch. Sam makes simple poles with nylon line and hooks and takes Ophelia down to the stream. He will teach her how to fish. Nearby, coconut trees provide some shade as they prepare their lines. After just an hour their small wicker basket is full of fish, still flapping. Ophelia smiles and laughs for the first time in many days.

'This is very good, Sam. We'll be able to take some back for dad and the others.'

'I'll take some back when I go over tonight, Phe.'

'Can I come with you, please?'

'Sorry, Phe. I need to move quietly. Things have changed. We're not safe in our own forest now. I'd better go alone. It'll be quicker.'

Ophelia nods resignedly. She can't argue with him. He is right. He usually is.

CHAPTER 4.

THE ASSAULT BEGINS

Sergeant Akemi Yoshito boards the troop transporter with a spring in his step. Action at last. He is impatient with the never-ending training, the drills, the discipline. Throughout his training, his instructors and officers have instilled a hatred of the Philippine people in him. Already, these people are less than human, they are 'the enemy' and he can't wait to kill them.

He joined the army five years ago. Straight from a youth offender's prison. Six months for breaking into a pensioner's home and robbing her. It was so unfair, he thought. She was old anyway, what did she matter? In the army interview he'd said he was really sorry – he'd learned his lesson. He'd put on his best 'sorry' face. Inside, he was laughing at how he was fooling them.

But now, he is proud. He stands in front of the mirror in the uniform his mum always cleans and irons, admiring his short haircut, his chiseled, clean-shaven features, and his slim build. He is going to fight his country's enemy. He can kill and be praised for it.

He waits for fifteen minutes at the airfield with the other men. All excited at the prospect of action at last. When the dull green plane finally rolls up, he and his comrades jostle to get onboard and find a space on the floor. There are no seats.

There is a pile of parachutes at the head of the plane, by the door. Each man will be given one just before he leaves – either by jumping, or, if they are reluctant, being pushed. Akime has never jumped before, there has been no time for any training. There is a small part of him that is frightened; he does not show it, even to himself.

He bunches in with a hundred other men, all silent, wrapped in their own thoughts. As he looks around, no one is making eye contact, no one is 'gung ho', no one is pumping themselves up ready for a battle. *What's wrong with these guys? They should be celebrating.* he thinks.

He is jarred back to reality by the jolt as the plane starts it's take-off run. Engines surge, it's too noisy to talk now even if he wanted to.

The journey is almost four hours. It is mostly silent. Three hours out, their commander, a young captain, steps to the front. Standing on top of the pile of parachutes, he calls them to attention.

'Get yourself ready, men. It's nearly time. Remember what we're fighting for.'

Akemi wishes so hard that he has the courage to stand up and say - 'We're with you, sir. We'll teach these ignorant savages.'

But he doesn't. The officer continues.

'Remember, we are doing this for the fatherland. We're here fighting for our Emperor, for our country, for our families, and above all, for our honor. Our deeds in this fight will be rewarded, either in this world or the next. Your country is already proud of you. Make them prouder today. Make your actions count.'

There is silence, no one looks at him. Akemi looks around. He sees fear on the faces of the young recruits. What is wrong with these cowards?

The officer dismounts his make-shift podium and blends back into the body of the plane. Still no one speaks,

The klaxon pierces the air, startling the troops. Large red flashing lights take life above the side exit door. No time for any more reflection. he jostles with his comrades to find a space as they all stand to form a line. The young lieutenant comes forward and details two men to stand by the door with hand gestures. It is futile to talk over the deafening sound, but everyone knows their job now.

Below them the country is in darkness; It is late at night here. It will be more difficult for locals to take pot-shots at them on the way down; they will organise and regroup under the cover of the night.

A rushing wind fills the compact aircraft cabin as the doors open inwards. Akemi then notices that the two men on exit hatch are each secured to the wall of the plane by a rope tied around a metal strut and their waist.

The first man steps forward, and the attendant fixes a pack to his back, taking care that it is properly secured, and attaches his rip cord to a hook inside to ensure that the chute opens, even if the frightened recruit doesn't do it himself. Then, with a pat on his back, the soldier disappears through the gaping hole into the dark night.

Akime is close to the back, so it will be a few minutes before his turn comes. He wishes it were over with. In his mind he sees himself on the ground, running towards the frightened, fleeing, enemy - bayonet fixed. There is no point wasting bullets on this scum.

Finally, he is face to face with the unsmiling men who strap his package on. It feels heavier than it had in training. The last thing he hears before the open sky consumes him, is his ripcord being secured with the dozens of others.

He has always avoided the 'scary' rides at the fairground, and now, here he is, plummeting towards the earth, hardly able to breathe, and at the mercy of the parachute packer, the winds, and gravity.

He loses consciousness briefly at the sudden jolt when he reaches the end of the ripcord and the white satin flies up from the backpack. As he descends, the wind is less fierce and as he comes round, he can see his comrades dotted around. Some are hitting the ground.

In the dim light he struggles to recognise the green fields, hedges, trees and the outlines of some buildings below. As the earth comes up to meet him, he sees cows, and a cowshed. They are going to land on a farm.

As far as he can tell, no one is shooting at them,

so they have the element of surprise. What should he do next? He struggles to recall the drill. Listen for the whistle and regroup is all he can remember – he hopes someone has the whistle.

Akemi hits the ground in a run, stumbles over a mole hill and gets dragged a hundred metres by the winds before he can undo the catches to release his chute. As the white pillows of silk disappear into the distance – carried by the wind, he remembers he is supposed to gather it up and conceal it. *No chance of that,* he thinks.

Looking around, he can see one comrade on either side, each struggling to draw up the chute material, but he hears no whistle. As he starts towards the nearest lad, he realizes there is a pain in his side. Looking down, he sees blood seeping through his clothes; a large thorn is embedded in his side. He winces as he pulls it out. It is not a serious wound, but still painful. He will look for iodine later; another reason to kill these bastards. He wouldn't be here if not for them.

'Are you ok, sergeant?'

The corporal stops folding his chute as he notices the blood on the uniform of the approaching man.

'Flesh wound. I'm fine. Who's got the whistle? Where do we go now?'

As a third colleague joins them, they hear a faint sound. A whistle, not far away, but the sound is not carried well on the winds. It seems to be coming from the right-hand side, maybe a few hundred yards in the distance.

'There's a group of trees over there.' He points to the middle ground ahead.

'Come on, lads. We need to keep on the move. No doubt the locals know we are here now so we should expect a response at any time. Fix bayonets. It's better we don't make a noise if we can help it.'

CHAPTER 5.

THE DEFENSE OF CEBU

Provincial Cebu is the busiest regional hub in the Central Visaya region. The capital city of the same name is the second largest city in the Philippines. The island is surrounded by over one hundred and fifty smaller ones. Developed by the Spanish from the sixteenth century onwards, it controls and facilitates trade and commerce throughout the country. The invading Japanese make it a major target in its ambitious conquest, second only to Manila.

The city barracks is home to a few hundred troops and sailors. In the large harbour, troop carriers and many smaller military vessels wait patiently preparing for battle.

Military bases are laid out in a triangle around Fort San Pedro which is next to the Basilica Minore del Santo Nino church The fort encompasses a large observation deck atop Mount Busay. Rising above the surrounding blocks, the tall building offers sweeping views over the city and out into the bay, with its busy shipping lanes. The deck is manned twenty-four hours by revolving teams of four men.

These days they don't have to rely on just their sharp eyes – they have radar, but it is still possible for the right aircraft to fly below a detectable level, so the first thing you know will be the far off specks in the sky getting bigger as they approach, as was the case only two hours ago.

After the recent events in America and Manila, the garrison has been bracing for the incursion for several days. The sight of several hundred planes approaching under the cover of a crescent moon still strikes fear in the military men manning their positions, most of whom have never seen conflict.

The planes are coming, that was for sure, but are they bombers? are they troop carriers? are they on their way to somewhere else?

The defenders soon have their answers. As the thundering flying warships approach, the sharp-eyed scouts see the side hatches open. They cannot spot the pin- prick dots of men falling out of the planes, but as the chutes unfurl, the skies became full of small white puffs. Hundreds fill the air like tiny exploding puffballs against the dark backdrop of a moonless sky, and there are still more coming.

Before the last ones hits the ground, the Philippine defenders are on the move. There is no point going out into the countryside to meet the invaders in a haphazard and open manner – that will cause massive casualties. Instead, defending troops will build barricades and defenses extending just beyond the town boundary.

The frantic defenders commandeer everything they can find. They hide in sheds, barns and other outbuildings. They use overturned barrows, carts, and anything else they can move; and then they wait.

Their scouts spot the invaders landing in open ground two miles out, to no resistance. In thirty minutes they can be at the town's perimeter; it will still be dark.

Two hundred or so Philippine soldiers hunker down, digging in where necessary, preparing for the assault.

Privately, those in command of the defenders know they cannot prevail. Even if they can hold the Japs at bay tonight, more will come. They keep a couple of hundred men back in the barracks to protect the townsfolk as best they can. Their commanding general is on the phone to headquarters in Manila.

'We estimate about three hundred of them sir, and they are dropping jeeps and supplies – it looks like ammunition – some boxes look like rocket launchers and grenades. They are certainly better equipped than us. Can we get some support, sir? We're likely to be overwhelmed. If we don't get help Cebu will fall.'

There is silence at the other end until a somber voice takes over. It's the deputy commander of the Philippine land forces.

'General, I'm sorry – there is nothing we can do for you. We don't have the resources ourselves. The Americans are still here and working with us, but we don't know for how long. Everyone here wants to fight – no one wants to give up. We've got to prevent Manila from falling. If we lose the Capital – we lose the country. What's the situation with the ships and the sailors?'

'They're still in port, sir, and the sailors are still here waiting for orders.'

'Get them out of the port, General. They must reach open waters as fast as they can. Get them out to sea. We don't want to give them to the Japs as a gift, do we?'

'Yes sir, right away.' He barks orders to a nearby subordinate.

'Anything else, sir?'

'Just do your best and try to hold on. If you can hold them back for just a few days maybe things will change. We have God on our side. Rally the troops and do the best you can. Good luck to you and all your men.'

With a 'click' the line goes dead.

On the front line, behind the barricades, the stone walls, and in the deserted barns and houses, the mood is grim but resolute. All eyes and minds are concentrated on the trees, ridges and roads in between the waiting troops and the oncoming invaders. All around the perimeter scouts are hiding in the woods, so they should get at least a few minutes warning.

In the center of Cebu, the commanding general meets with the town mayor.

The overweight man is panting from climbing the stairs to the military command post. He pats his sweating brow and sits in the nearest chair. It is thin and plastic – the general wonders whether it will hold his weight, it seems to strain but holds up.

'What are the arrangements for evacuating the V.I.P.s general? It's time we got out of here.'

'And who do you consider to be the V.I.P.s, Mr. Mayor?' He eyes the dislikable man with disdain.

'Well, the dignitaries. The councilors and their families, of course.'

The general sighs.

'Mr. Mayor. I'm not wasting my time on any evacuation plans – I'm here to defend the city and the people. I suggest you concentrate your efforts on keeping your people safe. We're not wasting scarce assets to save your ass. Get your 'V.I.P.s' together in a council meeting room and prepare to give yourselves up is my best advice.'

The mayor is taken aback by the tone of the military man.

'Excuse me, Mr. Mayor. I have a lot to do.'

Without waiting for a response, the general strides out of his room and down the stairs, leaving the mayor and his retinue behind.

Two miles away in the wooded area just beyond the city, the defenders are tense. It is two hours since they arrived and set up their defenses. For over an hour now, they've waited for the inevitable assault. Soldiers stopped dropping from the skies minutes before the local troops arrived in the area. Made up of mostly young conscripts, none of the defenders have seen battle before. Their anxious faces scour the trees and fields for signs of the approaching enemy. There are hundreds of them in the dips and thickets, When will they advance?

From their vantage point in the forests near about a quarter mile out, Akemi watches the defense preparation. Earlier, he and other officers had a briefing with their commander, Captain Yamoto.

'Sir, we're all ready. They're still building their defenses. Why don't we attack now before they're fully prepared?'

The older soldier eyes the keen sergeant as a teacher regards an insolent schoolboy.

'By the time we get there they will be ready. We wait a couple of hours; they are young and inexperienced. We'll let them become anxious, tired and frightened. They will be easy to overcome.'

Akira does not agree, but dare not say so, and his commander knows it. That was nearly two hours ago. At last the field radio rings. Akira gets the order he is waiting for.

'Proceed with the advance and engage.'

It is time.

Around him, he sees his comrades rise from the ditches, descend from the trees and crouch and crawl over the uneven terrain.

On the edges of the town some of the defenders spot the movement. A scout scurries back to the defenses. Something is happening.

Bushes twitch, small flocks of black birds rise into the sky startled by uniformed men advancing through the undergrowth. The invaders take advantage of the ground cover and bushes as long as they can.

There is a stretch of open field between the dense vegetation and the nearest defenses of the town. The plan is to get as up close as they can without exposing themselves, then pound the enemy with rapid fire and rockets for a minute or so, and while the local troops hunker down, they push forward to overrun them.

One or two defenders are complacent, stretching their heads up above the walls.

The first shot to be fired sends a young soldier flying backwards. Comrades either side watch wide-eyed as the doll-like body flies through the air to land prone on the ground, unmoving and staring upwards at the clear sky, a pool of deep red blood grows around his collar, a jagged section of flesh hanging down. The shell ricochets from his spine, opening half of his neck. Three spinal vertebrae are sticking out through the oozing and pulsating red mess.

More shots follow in quick succession and further down the line another man falls without the same theatrics as the first. The defenders get the message now and keep their heads down wherever they are; they know the enemy will be upon them anytime. All they can do is to wait, and hope.

Suddenly, with a 'boom' which shakes the

ground, a cowshed being used as a shelter explodes. Bricks and splintered wood fly outwards. One large stick goes through the leg of a nearby soldier as the building falls inwards onto the bodies of the three men inside.

Shouts and screams pierce the air as bullets and shrapnel find their marks in the flesh of terrified defenders.

Grenades and rockets now land frequently and the air becomes thick with smoke and the smell of burnt explosives.

The battle is frantic and bloody. Very few frontline defenders survive, and within twenty minutes only two thirds of the Philippino militia are still alive. From a safe bunker behind the front line, the general knows he is beaten. In fear of his own life, and to prevent further death, he orders the surrender. A sharp whistling sound fills the air and the soldiers still on their feet turn around to see a white flag tied to a stick being waved.

CHAPTER 6.
CONSOLIDATION.

The streets are quiet. Frightened townsfolk peer through their windows from behind the curtains. This is not how it is supposed to be.

'We're here to liberate them from their oppressive government. They will welcome us with open arms, that's what they told us.' One young conscript whispers to his friend as they march down the empty street.

Their officers told them they were liberators - freedom fighter for the oppressed. It doesn't feel like it. Stray dogs are the only things moving as the troop formations parade towards the city centre. There are no jubilant locals, no welcoming smiles.

The road to the government offices is uphill. As he looks back over his shoulder, Akime can see the flotilla of military and private boats, large and small, hurrying out of the harbor. They are heading for sanctuary in the ports of Malaysia. They can't know that within weeks Malaysia too will be overrun. Several larger vessels don't get away in time. They are still in the port and not going anywhere. He can see Japanese troops arriving at the docks and taking control.

Cohorts of the invading army fan out into the side streets as they advance to search for any remaining pockets of resistance, but Akime knows they will find little. The city had capitulated.

He marches resolutely along. In his heart there is joy, a sense of victory. The invincible troops of the emperor have beaten the local troops – he knows what is to come. He's heard comrades talk of what they will do to remnants of the army they find hiding. The helpless men will die in despair after watching their wives and daughters being used by the 'liberators'. He is looking forward to it.

In the mayor's office, the old man sits silently behind his desk awaiting the victors of the fight. He is flanked by half of his senior officials. The others have either fled the city or are in hiding.

His own escape plan was thwarted hours ago by his drivers and bodyguards who ran rather than risk their lives for the pompous fat man. His family went with his drivers and other staff, leaving him to face the invaders alone.

The Japanese commander marches solemnly into the room, stony faced; the timid officials rise but remain silent.

No words are spoken as the victorious officer strides around the desk and confronts the frightened mayor face to face. The sweating man backs away, and the general sits down in the mayor's chair. The occupiers set the tone.

'We don't want to kill people, mayor. Get the word out to your people that as long as they co-operate, they won't be harmed.' The mayor nods crisply but says nothing.

Captain Yamoto opens the folder he is carrying and hands the mayor a small white piece of paper.

'Here's a list of the hotels we will use for our accommodation. The occupiers have two hours to vacate them. Guests must leave immediately. The staff must stay to look after our men. I cannot vouch for their safety in case there are any guests still there when we take them over. We're occupying the army barracks as we speak. It is now a prison for captured troops, and other resistors.'

'Is there anything else... sir?' The fat man trembles as he speaks.

'We'll be using this building for administration, but you can stay to help us deal with any unrest. Find yourself another office nearby.' He nods at the other men in the room.

'You can all stay and assist the transition. Ok, go now. Attend to your jobs. All the services and transport will operate just as before. Make sure your townsfolk know that it is in their best interest to comply.'

He hands out sheets of paper to the assembled councilmen as they leave.

'These are permits signed by me. If any of my men approach you, show them these and they should leave you alone.'

Akime wakes early the next day, despite sleeping late. The noises from the next room kept him awake.

They were sounds of pleasure. Local girls will mostly give in, or even offer themselves in the hope of protection or favors.

He hadn't partaken of these 'activities' last night, he is sure he will later on, but right now it was the armed confrontations he was looking forward to, the killing.

He swings his legs over the side of the bed onto the ground and notices the piece of paper that has been slipped under the door. All the officers are summoned to a meeting in the mayors/captains office at ten o'clock. He looks at his watch. Eight am. Time for breakfast; he is hungry.

The formerly impressive mayor's chamber looks very different this morning. Walls are no longer covered with portraits of former mayors and councilmen. Instead, a framed portrait of the Japanese emperor adorns the tall wall at the end of the room. The mayoral desk is now jammed against the wall with a film projector resting on the corner and pointing at a white canvas screen erected at the front of the room, next to the emperor.

About thirty stacking chairs are set out in rows facing the screen.

As Akime sits down, he peers through the window. The skies overhead are filled with a dozen or more planes disgorging more paratroops to reinforce the occupation. He watches as the little parachute mushrooms open, dotting the skies.

As the room fills up, all conversation ceases. Flanked by two junior officers, the captain strides into the room and up to the front, he does not sit. An aide switches on the projector and a map of the southern Philippines appears on the screen. Facing the assembled officers, the commander addresses them – he is not one for small talk.

'Gentlemen, we've secured the capital, now it's time for the next part of the plan. If you look out of the windows, you will see fresh troops arriving from the motherland. More will arrive later today by ship now that the port is under our control. They will occupy the city and keep order. You are the more experienced leaders – the men under your command have more combat experience. Take your units and spread out into the surrounding countryside. Already we know that Philippine fighters have re-grouped in the forests. It won't be long until they start ambushing supply convoys or carrying out surprise attacks on out troops. We have to go out into the hills and villages to consolidate our control.'

He goes to the map on the wall. It has a dozen red markers dotted around the center of the city with arrows leading away from Cebu.

'You will see from the map where you're all going -I've prepared briefing packs for you.'

He hands around manila envelopes. Each has a different name on it.

Akemi sees his name on a star in the top right corner of the map – there is an arrow leading away from it towards Osamis. So that's where he's going. He waits until he is back in his room before opening the brown package. His instructions are concise and clear.

Your plane leaves for Osamis at eight a.m. tomorrow. You will land at Labo airfield, you will head towards the nearest town, Maranding, or you can commandeer local vehicles if there are any. Expect local resistance along the way, and check any villages you pass. Do not expect to be welcomed. When you get to Maranding, take command of the town. There is an American barracks there, but we expect it will be deserted. Commandeer whatever you need for accommodation and food. Take over the administration of the area and report back.

Our surveillance reports that are no longer any local or American troops in the city, so they don't expect any problems. The Mayor has signified he will surrender – when there is someone to surrender to. As soon as you have established control, leave men to maintain order and divide the rest of your men into groups. Spread out through the jungle in all directions to visit villages and other communities to ensure no bands of resistors are building up – the idea is to quash any resistance before it gets started.

The large troop transport plane is on the tarmac with its engine running when Akime arrives. His men are already boarding as he climbs aboard and takes charge. After twenty minutes the plane is full, all the soldiers are accounted for. Akime gives the order to take off for their one-hour journey into the mountainous jungle area.

◆ ◆ ◆

Gutting fish and preparing jungle vegetables is the daily routine for Ophelia and the other village women. So is watching the smoke trails overhead of military planes going past seven or eight times each day. The girls look up from their chores as the low hum of the plane's engines announce its arrival. This one is headed towards Maranding. Ophelia wonders what the Japanese soldiers on board are like. Surely they cannot be the monsters that some people say they are. They're human aren't they? They have families of their own back home. Ophelia feels sure that there will be a way to get along with them. It will not be long before she will find out.

Across the valley she sees wisps of smoke rising from her village. It is reassuring. Two miles away her father sits by the dying fire cooking the fish Sam brought the night before over the flames. A pot of vegetables simmers on the embers.

The walkie-talkie radio he now always carried with him crackles into life. It is Elmer from nearby Maranding.

'Hello? Yes, I can hear you. How are things

there? Any news?'

'Hello, my friend. The only news is not good. Japanese troops have landed. They're only a couple of hours away. Most able-bodied men have left the city, they're headed for the hills. They're talking about organizing a resistance, but many of us think it is futile. Our scouts say groups of the Japs are leaving the city and spreading out into the jungle. He saw one group coming our way but was not sure where it went.'

'We have seen no activity around here, Elmer. I'll warn the scouts and let you know if anything happens. What are you going to do?'

'The resistance fighters want to move up into the mountains and make camp. They plan to consolidate their position and hide from the Japanese. There are rumors of many atrocities in Cebu city. If they can stay free, they will help the local population in some way if they can. Some of my townsmen want to leave with them. I must let them go. If I were their age and with no responsibilities, I would be with them. But, like you, I cannot abandon the elderly and infirm here. I'll stay in the town and face whatever comes.'

Akime's group are not the first to arrive

at Maraming, They comandeer a large house abandoned by a wealthy family. They will rest for the night and set off into the jungle the next day.

A shaft of light appears through the dirty window telling him it is morning, but he's had little sleep. Throughout the night he heard shots ring out, usually followed by a scream either of a dying man or of his family. There were other screams, longer, and somehow more forlorn, as Japanese soldiers forced girls and wives alike to serve their new masters. Akime witnessed one such act just outside his house, A drunken soldier attacked an old man walking in the street for no reason at all, just sport. As he ran the man through with his bayonet, a woman, the daughter, ran out of a nearby house to tend to her dying father. The merciless soldier threw her to the ground and punched her while using her. He left her, naked, and sobbing, and lurched off down the road, singing.

As he looks out from his bedroom window, he can see the mountains in the distance. That is where he's going today. There are reports of resistance groups hiding close by in the jungle supported by local villages. They had to be stopped.

Akime can't wait to be out there, he wants to be fighting. In training, they were all assured that the enemy was merciless and evil. He's looking forward to ending the lives of as many soldiers and local sympathizers as he can, and he doesn't worry too much about the distinction between friend and foe. As far as Akime is concerned, all Philippino men are fair game, and most women too.

It is quiet now in the streets below; he smells eggs cooking as he rises and packs, ready for the onwards journey to… God knows where.

The Japanese army is nothing if not efficient, and his transport wagon appears as he and his men finish breakfast. A messenger brings final orders from the hurriedly set up command center just before they depart. The shuddering engine makes it difficult to read the papers, but he can understand what he needs to. Villagers should be 'persuaded' to tell him where the camps of the resistance fighter are. There is a list. Mabuhay is on it.

They land at a deserted U.S.army landing strip which is deserted.

In sweltering heat, they advance through the jungle for most of the day; the going is difficult. If they are lucky there is a track to follow, if not, they are cutting their way through dense vegetation; by the evening they see the lights of the small village across the valley.

'Can we go in, sir? We need to deal with them, they might run away during the night.'

Akime spoke to his commanding officer over the radio.

'No sergeant, the men are all tired. Little will be lost if we wait until tomorrow. And remember sergeant, we're only 'liquidating' soldiers who don't surrender, and their sympathisers.

'Surrender, sir? And what do we with them if they surrender? We've nowhere to keep them, and nowhere to take them.' The officer ignores the comment.

'You have your orders sergeant, get the camp organized. Eat cold rations. I don't want any fires tonight.'

The burly man wanders off, happier than at the start of the call. There are no plans for taking and detaining prisoners. Their superiors did not expect any. As far as the sergeant is concerned, he has the green light now to kill any Philippino he meets. Akime smiles to himself. Tomorrow will be a good day.

CHAPTER 7.

ATROCITIES CONTINUE

Pedro scampers into the village as fast as he can. For ten years old, he is quick. The boy refused to leave when the others did as he wanted to look after his sick grandmother. His parents both succumbed to dengue fever when he was five years old. The old lady had looked after him ever since.

He runs straight into Celmar's hut.

'They're here.' he pants.

'They've set up camp a mile down the road. It looks like they're settling down for the night.'

The village captain looks up into the sky. It is nearly dark. They might come tomorrow.

'Don't worry, child. Check on your grandmother. We'll prepare for them in the morning.'

As soon as the boy leaves, Celmar calls Elmer.

'They're here, my friend. They're camped just down the road. I expect they'll come into the village in the morning. There's only me here with the elderly and inform – we're hardly a threat to them. I'll give them food. Things will be fine, Elmer. We'll get through this. I'll call you tomorrow.'

'Okay, Celmar, whatever you do, don't show any resistance. Our lives mean nothing to them. I've got to go. I don't want them to find this radio. Take care of yourself.' The line goes dead.

Celmar has visibly aged over the past few weeks and is anxious and tired. He doesn't contact Ophelia, she will only worry, and there is nothing she can do. He readies himself to sleep, but he tosses and turns, unsettled, and fearing what the dawn will bring.

The young boy is not the only one to observe the arriving militia. From an adjacent ridge, Sam spots the enemy camp as he slips through the undergrowth. He is on the way to check on the village and Celmar, but he stops when he spies the soldiers clearing trees and setting up equipment . He goes straight back to the hillside encampment with the news.

'It looks like there are about ten of them, all well-armed. They're bedding down for the night. Try not to worry, Phe, Celmar won't show any resistance if they show up, and they'll see there's nothing there for them.'

Ophelia bites her lip and holds back tears. All they can do is wait and see.

For the worried girl, the night passes slowly. Slight breezes do little to reduce the sweltering jungle heat, but that is not the only thing causing Ophelia to doze restlessly. She tosses and turns until the lightening skies herald the morning.

The sun is rising at the horizon as she makes her way down to the stream to wash. She thinks of her father.

At that moment he is feeding the animals, a little earlier than usual. He too had not slept well in apprehension of what the day might bring. He does not have to wait long to find out.

As they approach, he spies them. Three young soldiers moving along the dirt track into the village, their eyes darting everywhere, expecting resistance.

The old village captain stands by the pigpen and smiles as they near – he opens his hands to show he is unarmed and struggles to maintain his smile, all three men have their guns raised and fixed on him. Three other men now came into view, a sergeant and two other youths. The soldiers have more courage in moving forward now; it seems like there is just one helpless old man. The six surround the village elder and lower their weapons, realising there is no threat.

Sergeant Akemi glances around. So, there are a couple of pigs and goats – and he hears chickens. They'll have a nice haul to take back – the men will eat well today.

'Check all the tents. Search for weapons, be wary in case any fighters are hiding; you better go in pairs.'

He turns to the nearest man.

'You. Stay with me,'

The other four lads scurry off.

Surprised shouts and screams come from the huts as the lads enter without warning. The elderly occupants fear the worst. Celmar pleads with the sergeant.

'Please, sir. There's no need to be rough with us. We are poor, simple people. There are no fighters here. Most people left a while ago. I stayed because I am the village captain, they rest are too old or too sick to travel. They are my responsibility.'

As he speaks, out of the corner of his eye, he sees the young boy who acted as a lookout earlier slip from the back of the furthest hut into the bushes behind, unseen. Celmar was glad he'd got away. It is beginning to look as if these men may not treat them well.

Celmar learned to speak English when he was young. He knows his visitors will not speak Bisayan, his native tongue, so he speaks in English, hoping that one of them might also know the language.

The sergeant ignores his protestations, but then speaks to him in passable English.

'We're taking your livestock, old man. Our men need to eat. Gather up the chickens and any other food you have. We'll use your cart to take it back.'

He gestures to the old wagon which Celmar used to go to other villages, then he realises something else.

'Wait a minute. If you have a wagon, you must have a horse. Find it and hitch it up to the wagon, and I'll be watching you. If you run, I'll shoot you and everyone else here.'

Before the old man can do the sergeant's bidding, the other soldiers return from the huts carrying some machetes.

'Why do you have weapons, you said you were peaceful? You lied to me.'

He shoved the old man to the ground.

'Sir, they're not for fighting. They're for farming and hunting. That's how we live, sir, we need them, or we'll starve.'

'Well, you'd better find another way to live. We're keeping these, now, get the food loaded on the wagon. You can drive it.'

He turns to the men who are just standing around.

'Help him then, or we'll be here all day,'

Two of the recruits walked off with the old man to help him.

It takes about an hour to load the wagon; then the group is ready to leave.

'I beg you sir, please can you leave just a little of the food? You've seen the old women and the sick in the tents. They're too weak to get their own food. They'll die without help. Please let me keep some back.' Celmar puts his hands together in supplication.

The sergeant glances at his men.

'We wouldn't want these old villagers to starve, would we? You'd better take care of them.'

He smiles at his lads as they nod and walk away.

Celmar does not realise what is going on until he is shaken by two sharp rifle cracks, then a further three, coming from the huts.

'There now. You don't have to worry about feeding them anymore.'

A couple of his men laugh.

Celmar is silent, not daring to speak and unable to believe what is happening. His worries about these evil men are now confirmed. He realises too, that they will kill him as soon as he is no use to them unless he can think of something.

Still in a daze, Celmar hitches the horse to the wagon and climbs up to take the reins.

Led by the sergeant, and with the other men behind, the small convoy set off with Celmar driving the food wagon. The villagers do not usually make the old horse carry such a heavy load. As it strains harder, the overloaded cart moves.

Ever vigilant for an ambush, the group moves out of the village slowly along the track, taking about thirty minutes to get back.

When they reach the camp. The other soldiers watch them process into the centre of the clearing.

'Put this one to work. He can act as a scout, and maybe he can cook some of this food for us, but shoot him if you have any trouble.' Akemi regards Celmar who sits atop the wagon.

'He's the village elder. I thought he may as well deliver the food he donated to us.'

One of his men smirks at the remark.

'What about the rest of the villagers, sir?'

'They resisted us, and they had weapons.'

He produces the two machetes his men found.

'We had no choice, they could have passed information to the enemy after we left'

Some men look down at the machetes. They know what Akemi did was wrong, but they dare not go against him.

Sam and Ophelia with a couple other lads creep through the vegetation towards their village. It is midday, and Sam cannot raise Celmar on the radio. Sam usually goes alone, but today Ophelia insists on coming.

They do not go directly. That would take them too close to the Japanese encampment. They circle around, moving slowly and always warily.

From a distance the camp looks peaceful, but deserted. As they ease closer, they notice it is unusually quiet. There are no animals anywhere. The paddock gates are wide open and there isn't the usual sound of chickens and goats they would expect. They can see that two huts have doors forced in. Not daring to shout out, they creep into the village through a side lane and look into the first hut they pass. It seems that the soldiers have ransacked all the buildings, but the first hut appears empty now. As they move onto the second one, they hear a faint mew, like a distressed cat. Moving into the shack, they find an old lady laying on bloody sheets on a bamboo bed resting against the wall. Ophelia rushes to her.

'Oh, my dear Lola, what happened here?'

The old woman is too far gone to make much sense, but she smiles a little as Ophelia squeezes her hand.

Sam gently pulls back a blood-soaked sheet revealing a bullet hole in her chest, and from the blood on the ground under the bed, Sam knows there was an exit wound behind. She didn't die instantly as the round didn't shatter inside – it travelled straight through.

Unfortunately, it has nicked her lung which is slowly filling up with blood, she is gasping for breath now. She is over eighty years old and very frail. Sam knows she will never rise from her bed again.

Although her eyes are not open, she knows someone is there. She tries to mumble something, but it is impossible to understand. Sam shakes his head as Ophelia looks at him, she holds the old lady's hands.

'It's alright Lola, we're here now. Just rest and relax. You'll feel better soon.'

Ophelia is frightened but tries not to show it. The invaders could return at any time. She has never been in a position like this before and doesn't know what to say – anyway, what she is saying nearly true, the old woman will soon feel no more pain. The old lady is struggling to sit up, but the movement opens the gaping wound on her side. More blood spills out onto the dirt floor.

'Japs... killers... nobody left...'

Ophelia can only just make out the whispered sounds, but now, there are no more words from the old lady, just a wretched faint gasp, like a deflating balloon, and then she is still. She looks for all the world as if she is sleeping, but there are no chest movements. She is gone.

Ophelia is still clinging to the her frail hands.

Short sobs are coming silently as a tear runs down her cheek. Lola has been like a grandmother to all the young folk in the village, Sam pulls her aside.

'Come on, Phe, we need to hurry. Get all the stuff together to take back to the camp. Check for any animals. I doubt there's anything of value left but check to be sure.'

'Is it safe, Sam? What if they come back?' Sam nods.

'We must be quick, Phe.'

He needs to keep her busy to stop her panicking, and is keen to get away in case the soldiers return. They must search the other huts without her. He expects to find her father's body and does not want her there when he does.

In the next house along, the only thing in the otherwise empty space is a pile of rags and sheets in the corner. Sam is about to leave when a slight movement in the corner catches his eye; the rags are moving. Cautiously, he lifts the corner of a sheet; two beady eyes look up at him. As Sam pulls the cover away the gaping, frightened face stares up at him. It is the lad who escaped during the visit of the Japs. The trembling boy recognizes Sam and runs to him, hugging him so tightly it seems like he will never let go. Sam pushes him away but still holds the boy's shoulders.

'It's ok, Pedro. You're safe now. We'll take you into the mountains with us, nobody can hurt you there.'

The boy sobs and holds the young man's arms

tight. Sam comforts him for a while, then takes him outside. Ophelia sees him come out with the boy and rushes over.

'Pedro? I'm so glad you're okay.' she holds the boy tightly and strokes his hair.

'I ran into the forest and hid until they left. The forest is safer than the village; I was too frightened to come back for a long time, then I hid when I heard noises.'

The boy is calmer now, but still holds tightly to Ophelia.

'Look after the lad, Phe. He'll be okay, just reassure him – we'll take him to the camp with us.'

Ophelia leads Pedro away, holding his hand.

There are three more huts to search; Sam finds the bodies of the other old villagers. It is not safe to stay to bury them, so he covers them as best he can and leaves them. The Japanese have taken anything of value or use. Once he is sure there are no more bodies or other surprises, Sam joins Ophelia who, with Pedro, is trying to catch two chickens running scared in the square.

'There's no one else here, Phe. We've checked everywhere, and the horse and wagon have gone.'

Ophelia stops chasing a chicken. Sam takes her to one side.

'There's no sign of your dad, Phe. They must have taken him with them. All the food and supplies are gone. It looks like they made him drive the wagon back to their camp.'

The girl is still in shock, looking at what has

become of her village and her people. She tries to hold back tears, but wells up as she looks at Sam.

'Do you think he's still alive?' she gazes up at him pleadingly, as if he can tell her what she aches to hear.

'Yes, I do.' Sam nods.

'If they were going to kill him, why not just do it here? I'm sure they took him away for a reason. I think he's still alive, sweetheart. Tomorrow, I'll take a few guys and check out the camp – see if we can't find something out.

CHAPTER 8.

THE RESCUE

Sergeant Akime leads the way back into the camp, sitting behind Celmar on the horse and cart. After a while, Celmar spots some activity ahead. Sweaty Japanese soldiers have their shirts off in the tropical heat. They are clearing the undergrowth. Ahead, there is a clearing where many smaller ones have already been felled. Other soldiers are building rudimentary huts and lean-tos. Celmar smiles at their amateurish efforts. These are conscripts who have never lived in a forest; they are not at home, and it shows.

The village captain looks around him. These are more boys than men, he judges their average age to be less than twenty. An older man spits at him in disdain as they pass by.

'Take the wagon over there.' snaps Akime, pointing to a cleared area between the huts.

The undergrowth now opens up to give way to a large, cleared area.

Celmar looks over at a roughly built stockade with a roof of banana leaves set back in front of him on the left. If he were not so frightened, he would have laughed at the structures, barely holding together and built without skill. They pull up beside one of the larger huts.

'Put all the food in there. When you've finished,

tie the horse up to the fence. Stay with the wagon so we can see where you are; if you try to run, we'll shoot you. We might keep you alive if you're useful to us, so don't cause any trouble.'

Celmar nods. He wants to survive, and now thinks he has a chance. After he is done, he looks around. Soldiers are sat smoking, playing cards, and laughing. A few of the soldiers sit cleaning their weapons or washing; all are monitoring him. He dares to ponder an escape but realises his chances are slim. Maybe the other men of the village will come to rescue him.

There is one tall tree left standing in the centre of the camp. The soldiers use it to fix their radio transmitter in the branches. They bind a rope to Celmar's left leg and tie the other to the tree, with about twenty feet of slack.

'We'll give you wood and a pot – you can make a meal with the stuff we brought back. You can cook, can't you?' Celmar nods. He doesn't dare to say no. Akima sends two men to guard him. They have to give him a knife to prepare the food, but they don't want him to cut through the rope and escape.

Celmar has never cooked a meal, ever. Others have always prepared food for him. First his mother, then later his wife. He sets about building the fire and skinning and slicing the vegetables. All the time trying to look as if he knows what he is doing. Trembling, he tries to remember what his wife does, knowing his life depends on the results of his labours. Hoping he can convince them, he throws the chopped vegetables into the pot with the water, making sure the fire underneath does not go out. He remembers his wife always adds salt and throws some in, hoping it will impress his captors. Next to the pot he cleans a metal sheet and puts it over the flames, then lays the only slab of pork on top. To his satisfaction, it starts to sizzle.

After maybe thirty minutes, steam rises as the water boils. The meat smells good and is darkening and crisping nicely. When he considers the vegetables and meat is ready, he tells the guards they can eat now. They need not be told twice. The hungry conscripts take the knives away from Celmar and call all the others over.

Later, after their meal, Celmar clears everything away and cleans the plates. Some men sit around drinking and laughing for a while, and then settle down in the makeshift huts for the night, leaving Celmar still tied to the pole. The rope will not allow him to reach even the nearest hut. After clearing a space, he lies down in the dirt and his thoughts drift to his family. Are they still alive? Will he ever see them again? Will he survive tomorrow? Sleep is again driven away by his fears.

◆ ◆ ◆

Ophelia captures two chickens and returns to the village with them in a sack. After eating mainly vegetables for so long, the fowl are a welcome addition to the meagre meal Ophelia's mother and her friends are preparing.

They take their food in silence as they learn of the devastation of their village, and the slaughter. The only sounds come from some people who have lost relatives in the Japanese attack and cannot hold back sobs.

After the meal, Sam takes Ophelia to one side – two of his friends join them.

'We've been talking, Phe. We're going to get your dad tonight. It's not safe to wait longer. They'll only keep him alive as long as they need him; these soldiers don't take prisoners. It has to be tonight; tomorrow may be too late.'

Secretly, Sam worries that they may already be too late, but he will not tell Ophelia that.

'We'll scout out the camp and find out where they are keeping him, and the best way to free him. If we get there around three a.m. most of them will be asleep, but I'm sure they'll post lookouts. We must be careful. It's just the three of us going, so we can move quickly. Soon after midnight will be the best time to leave, plenty of time to approach cautiously.

'I'll come with you. I'm fast, I can help,' offers Ophelia.

Sam shakes his head.

'You can't Phe, you'll hold us up. We'll be looking out for you and it will distract us. Anyway, we only have three guns, and you can't go unarmed. A knife will be no good against these vicious men.'

'Ophelia sighs – she can't argue with their logic. Sam looks at his watch and speaks to the others.

'Let's get a few hours sleep. We'll meet back here at midnight. We need to prepare.'

Ophelia settles down to rest, but she can't sleep. She shuts her eyes, but her brain will not be quiet. Her mind wanders back to better times. The meat they ate earlier reminded her of parties and celebrations in the village where everyone put on their best clothes and ate chicken, roast pork, and fresh fish. Her eyes moisten as she wonders if there will ever be any parties like that again. Eventually she nods off but wakes at midnight as she hears the boys preparing outside her hut.

The young men busy themselves checking the two rifles and one revolver. They are old, but they still work. Sam and the boys are good shots, but if they have to use them tonight, it won't be for the wild pig, halo lizards and birds they are used to shooting. Each man carries a machete at the waist and a short knife. Between them they only have twelve bullets. Sam gathers them together and distributes the ammunition.

'There are just three of us, lads – and there are more than ten of them, so everything depends on surprise and speed. Don't use the guns unless you have to.'

They finish their preparations in the cooler air and quiet of the night.

During the day, the forest abounds with the

shrieks of the howler monkeys and the different calls of the birds, but at night it is more sedate. Night animals, the owls, the anteaters, the sloths, are quieter. The only sounds are the light breeze rustling through the trees and groups of crickets rasping in the trees.

The three quietly leave the encampment around one a.m. and tack their way through the dense jungle. When they are just under a mile from the enemy camp, they slow down – it is time to be more vigilant.

They expect that the troops will post sentries around the camp to look out in case of an attack, but Sam and his friends are more experienced than the foreign soldiers in this environment. The jungle is their home. They can move silently through the dense undergrowth, while the soldiers are slow and clumsy.

Every hundred yards the tallest lad shins up a tree to gain a better vantage. About three hundred yards out from the camp, they spot the first guard. He is nestled in a bush set back against a rocky outcrop. He appears to be asleep – the guards are not expecting trouble.

The boys scout all around the sleeping camp. They discover that the inexperienced soldiers have only posted three lookouts. Each is stationed just beyond the perimeter of the camp in different directions to form a triangle around the camp. Two are dozing, but still awake. One is fast asleep, curled up on his rug. He is the easiest, he will be the first.

Sam sneaks up on the man's blind side and withdraws his short knife. He sidles along the ridge to get up beside him. When he is up close, he firmly clasps his right hand over the man's mouth to stop him making a sound and jerks his head back hard, breaking his neck and exposing his throat. Sam has never killed a man before, but he knows it must be done. It's just like killing a pig, he tells himself. The sharp knife goes in at the front and to the side. There is only a gurgle from the surprised man. Blood comes from his neck in strong spurts, so Sam knows he's found the artery. He holds his hand tight over the man's mouth until he feels the body go limp, then takes his hand away from the gaping mouth. There is no breath.

The three then move around the perimeter to the next guard. He appears relaxed, but he has his eyes open. They must be more careful.

'I'll take this one,' says the tall lad who'd climbed the tree.

'He's awake, I think two of us need to do this.' Sam explains how they will kill him – the others nod.

From a distance they watch him. The man sits, propped up against a tree. If they don't make a sound, it should be easy to get close to him. Both men approach the tree, one man with his knife out and Sam holding his machete, ready. The Japanese soldiers are not used to the oppressive heat – this one has taken his jacket off and sits there just in his shirt. This is an advantage.

They are just a two metres from the guard now, but out of sight of him behind the tree. The two attackers nod at each other.

The one with the short knife moves around the tree and lunges, pushing the dagger deep into the man's side, just below the ribcage. Swiftly, he moves the knife from side to side to maximise the damage. The startled man grunts with surprise, but before he can cry out, Sam's machete hits him in the neck two inches below the jaw with such force that it severs his head from his body. The head falls sideways and rolls a few feet while the body slumps forward with blood pumping from the neck.

The three regroup around the dead lookout.

'Do we have to do the third one? He's on the other side of the village. Maybe we can sneak into the village, find Celmar, and get him away without the other troops knowing.'

Sam frowns.

'No, we must kill him. We have the advantage now, but once we're closer, we'll be exposed – we need all the help we can get.'

The other boys nod in agreement.

'Come on, let's get it done, same way as last time, okay?'

The boys set off circling the camp, making their way round to the last guard. The practice helped – it is easy this time, but instead of decapitation, Sam slits the man's throat and he slumps to the ground. With the three guards out of the way they are free to approach the camp. As they get closer, they see the outlines of the rudimentary huts, lit by the dying embers of the campfire on which Celmar earlier cooked the food.

The fire also lights a still form lying just feet away, curled up on the ground. Celmar is not asleep, he lays resting with his eyes open, scouring the vegetation just yards away for any movement.

The boys spot the still figure from about ten yards out. There seems to be no-one else around – the other men must be in the make-shift huts. For the raiders, things are going well so far. The rest of the Japanese are asleep inside the huts, relying on the now dead lookouts to warn them of any danger.

Sam creeps towards Celmar who is now wide awake and alert. Neither man speaks while Sam cuts the rope attached to the old man's leg. The other two men watch from the bushes for movement from the huts or the sleeping enemy as Sam and Celmar move towards the edge of the camp. Just as they reach the first bush a large black bird rises squawking from the undergrowth, disturbed by the boy's movement. That is all it takes. Through the open door of the nearest hut, one soldier opens an eye and sees movement, as his vision clears, he sees the men moving towards the forest. His rifle is within inches of his searching hand and within seconds it is at his shoulder. The shot wakes the camp and others call out to each other and get to their feet. The first shot misses, but his vision is focusing better. A second bullet embeds itself in Celmar's right thigh, and he sinks to the ground, screaming in pain. Sam tries to lift him.

'No, leave me – you can't help me. You must help the others – get back to the rest of the villagers – it's too late for me.' Celmar winces as he pushes Sam's hand away.

'Quickly, get away while you can.' The other two rescuers pull Sam away from the old man and further into the bush. The Japanese troops realise what is happening and start moving towards the group. One soldier whose bullet hit Celmar reaches the injured man and lifts his rifle to finish the job. He starts to squeeze the trigger until he hears sergeant Akime approach and shout.

'No, don't kill him. I have other plans.'

Other men rush into the bushes to chase the escaping boys.

'Wait, don't bother chasing them. They're more experienced and faster than you in this jungle – I have a better idea.'

Akime Stands over the prone Celmar and puts a foot on his bleeding wound, grinding the heel into the damaged muscle and causing the unfortunate man to cry out in agony.

'There's not much blood.' observes the sergeant. 'You didn't hit an artery. He'll last for a few hours. Drag him back to the village. Tie him up again, although I don't think he'll be going very far, but just in case. You two! Come with me – bring machetes – and a rope.'

CHAPTER 9.

COPING WITH DEATH.

Breathlessly, Sam and his friends hurry away from the Japanese camp, slowing down a little when they realise they are not being followed. The sun is rising above the distant mountains as they stumble back into the encampment. Ophelia is waiting.

'Sam? Are you okay? What happened. What happened to my dad?' She rushes to him, helping him into the clearing.

'I'm sorry, 'Phe. We couldn't get him away. They shot him in the leg as we were leaving. He couldn't walk. There was nothing we could do.' Ophelia is crying now.

'Don't lose hope 'Phe. I think he may still be alive. They didn't shoot him again. We didn't hear a gunshot, and his wound is not bad enough to kill him. Perhaps we can try again later.'

Sam's words do not help now. Ophelia runs to her mother who is coming forward. As the young girl tells her mother the news the old lady hugs her daughter, sobbing.

'We'll let things settle down for a few hours, 'Phe, then we'll go back and find out what's happening – I know it's difficult, but try not to lose hope.' Ophelia nods through her tears.

◆ ◆ ◆

Akime surveys the efforts his men are making. They are fixing a four metre long felled coconut tree trunk between two other tall trees about three metres apart and clearing away the bushes to create a small clearing.

'Fix it about five metres off the ground.' He bellows. The fit young conscripts can easily shin up the trees to fix the felled tree between them. Akime throws the rope over the centre of the middle tree and is pleased when both ends reach the ground.

'Go and fetch the old man, and one of the empty oil drums.' He folds one end of the rope over and starts to make a noose.

A few moments later, several of his troops return, dragging the village captain through the bushes by the rope still attached to him. The old man grunts as they dump him at the feet of the sergeant. Celmar is confronted by the noose hanging over a branch – it is obvious what they are planning. Akine is pleased when he sees a look of horror come over the old man's face.

'What do you want to do with the drum, sir?' the young lad asks as he rolls it into the clearing.

Akime picks up a hammer they'd used to make the rudimentary gallows. He hits the top of the oil drum. The metallic clang resonates through the air and the bushes, birds fly up in distress and small monkeys scatter into the undergrowth in panic.

The other soldiers look at their leader curiously as he strikes the drum again.

'We're going to make an example of this one.' He

says, kicking the old man in the legs.

'I want to show the locals what happens when they defy us.'

He hands the hammer to a junior soldier.

'Keep banging the drum – every few seconds – let's drum up an audience. I want these jungle monkeys to watch this and spread the word. They have the advantage of knowing the forest, it's easy for them to get around quietly and conceal themselves. They'll hide in the bushes and trees to watch. We might not see them, but I know they'll be there. Keep up the drumming, they'll come soon. We'll give them time.'

Back in the village, Sam and Ophelia are planning to return to the army camp in the evening after the light dims when they hear the noise. 'Tang…' it is a loud resounding sound, like a giant tin bell. All activity and conversation stops. No-one has ever heard anything like it. Before anyone speaks it comes again, 'Tang…', then a third time. It seems to come every five seconds or so, and it does not stop.

'Come on, we must find out what's happening.' A few of the younger and fitter villagers follow Sam and Ophelia into the forest towards the sound.

'Wait a minute,' says Sam. 'It's coming from the direction of the Japanese soldiers – we must proceed carefully.'

The sound gets louder as they get deeper into the jungle, and closer to the enemy camp. They spread out to ensure they are not seen, they are now within a kilometre of the camp. Sam spots some movement a long way away and hunkers down to see better but the bushes are too thick. He shins up a nearby tree to get a better view.

There are a few soldiers mingling in a space

around two small trees. He can see the crosspiece formed by the felled tree and a small figure huddled up like a foetus on the ground. With horror, he realized that the huddled body is Celmar, and there is a rope strung over the felled tree tied into a noose. Sam moves back closer to Ophelia and holds her hand.

The group move back together carefully, ensuring they cannot be noticed, but they can clearly see the scene unfolding in the distance.

Celmar is still awake and his leg is no longer bleeding, but his trousers are soaked with blood which is now mostly dry. Akime looks around him, at the three youngest members of his group.

'Lucas, Fritz, Klaus, get over here.' The three quickly snap to attention and run to their commander.

'Pull him to his feet.' The three lift the limp old man and stand him on his feet. The other man has been hitting the oil drum for thirty minutes now, Akime motions him to stop.

'That's enough. They'll be here by now. We may not see them, but I know they are there.'

Akime faces away from the camp. He stands on a log to give himself some height and shouts into the forest.

'We know you're there. We know you're watching. I want you to see what happens when you go against the Imperial Japanese Army.'

He turns towards Celmar and the three holding him, Slowly, for theatrical effect, he picks up the noose from the ground and hands the other end to the soldiers holding the old man.

'Okay, pull him up.' The lads look at each other, none of them wants to be the first to move.

Akime looks angry and takes his pistol from its

holster.

'Do it now, or it will be you instead.' He raises the gun.

The three lads slowly begin to pull the rope until it is tight, and Celmar is stood on his toes.

'Keep going, come on. I want him three feet off the ground for everyone to see,'

As the old man is lifted slowly into the air by the neck he begins to gurgle and grasps at his neck. Death will not be fast.

A hundred metres away Sam struggles to keep Ophelia quiet. His hand is over her mouth and he needs all his strength to prevent her from rising, screaming, and running towards the morbid scene.

The Japanese soldiers watch the old man as he writhes and twitches, smiling at the look of agony on his face, which is slowly turning purple. His eyes bulge and after about five minutes his efforts become less. He is now still, and dangling, swaying gently.

Sam drags her away before the end. There is no point in waiting. It is agony for Ophelia and her mother to see the cruel spectacle.

'Ophelia, love, there is nothing we can do for him. We'll go back in a few hours. If we can get his body we'll give him a proper funeral. You need to be strong now, there's your mother to think about.'

Ophelia says nothing. She is curled up, the tears have dried up now. Instead, she moans and cries like a baby.

Akime inspects the hanging body.

'Okay, lads you can let him go now.'

Lucas, Fritz, and Klaus release the rope and Celmars dead body collapses to the ground.

'Are you sure he's dead, sir?' asks Lucas.

'Well, let's make sure, shall we?"

Akime draws his short sword and plunges it into the still body. There is no movement, but blood begins to ooze out of the wound onto the dirt.

'Should we bury him, sir? asks Fritz.

'No need. The animals will dispose of the flesh soon enough. Why waste our energy?' replies Akime, wiping his sword on the undergrowth.

'Come on, lads. Let's get back to camp.' He looks at Fritz, Klaus and Lucas. 'You three killed him, so you can cook breakfast.' He laughs as he sets off through the bushes.

They take the noose from around his neck, gather up their equipment and set off after their leader. Celmar's body now lies alone in the middle of the clearing. There is no noise, and the air is still. He looks asleep, peaceful now, but the wound in his side continues to release dark, thick blood onto the hot, dry ground.

Two hours later, the soldiers are long gone. No blood comes from the body now. The wound is dry, there is s wide dark patch on the ground where the blood has spilled.

A barely discernable wisp of something comes from the dark patch. It looks a little like smoke, or mist, but there is a faint smokey glow appearing around Celmar. The forest, usually loud and very active at this time of day, becomes quiet and still. It is as if the animals and birds can sense something unusual; something sinister is happening.

It is the middle of the day, the sun is at it's hottest, but suddenly, a coldness invades the area. The uncanny chill emanates from the lifeless body and extends to the edge of the clearing.

More 'smoke' rises from the ground. It is white, but an unusual white. There are flashes, sparks within it and a low cracking sound can be heard in the quiet hearing.

The smoke becomes a cloud and now engulfs the body, and is still rising. When the now thick mist is about two metres above the body and still rising, it starts to take shape. No longer a bulbous mass, discernable features begin to form. Ghostly legs and feet take shape at the bottom, and eerie, spindly arms now protrude from the cloud with bony twig-like fingers.

At the top, a bulbous head sits on misty shoulders. It is about the size of the head of a child of maybe ten or eleven. No ears are discernable, but a thin line forms the outline of a ghoulish mouth – it opens. As the lips part, a deep darkness within is apparent. It is black, blacker than anything you can imagine, and it is deep. It is like looking into the depths of space, a very lonely, dark, and frightening space.

No nose is yet discernable, but pin pricks of deep dark, red light herald the formation of eyes; still small, they are piercing and ominous.

As the whole unworldly being takes shape, the eyes start to bulge, and a curious smell surrounds the area. A bit like rotting fish, but with a tinge of sweetness, and of bitterness. Is is a primeval smell that no person has ever smelled, and survived.

Now fully formed into a shimmering human-like shape, the apparition rises. The mouth opens wider, as if in a scream, and the ruby eyes cast down to the body below. The crackling sound increases as the inhuman and other-worldly form rises up, then dives down into the body of Celmar, and through, into the ground below. And then it is gone.

Stillness continues for a few more moments, and then some animals dare to chirp, to cry out, to scurry around, and the temperature slowly rises. In two hours, things are back as they should be. There are no witnesses to the ghostly appearance, but it's coming does not end there. It will not be forgotten. It will affect many lives, and end a few.

The Santilmo has come. Celmar's death in such inhuman and monstrous circumstances, and leaving a traumatised young daughter and a grieving wife, will have consequences for those who partook in this evil deed.

The Santilmo knows no time. No limits. Called into existence by the dastardly, cruel and inhuman deeds of evil men, it will first appear, then disappear, as quickly as it arose, but it is not gone. It is there, watching and waiting while the world goes on around it.

It will watch, and wait, until the moment is right. It could be hours, or it could be days, months or even years. But, it will not give up, it will not forget, until it's work is done.

A short distance away in the villagers temporary home, the Santilmo manifests, but it cannot be seen. It has the choice to be visible or to hide itself. Most people need not be frightened by it's appearance.

Ophelia lies on her bed staring into space. She is past tears, but her body heaves with uncontrollable sobbing still. She is alone. Sam stayed with her for a long time, then left her to rest. The Santilmo rises beside her bed, unseen, touches her shoulder with a spindly finger, then is gone.

Ophelia slowly ceases her sobs, and drifts into a quiet sleep. Sam looks in on her and is pleased to see her asleep. It will do her good. They will not wake her.

She sleeps for most of the day, but wakes in the

early evening when the smell of cooking is in the air. She is hungry.

From a distance, Sam sees her appear at the entrance to the tent and rushes over.

'How are you feeling, Oph'?'

She smiles at him weakly.

'I'm feeling better, Sam. Calmer now. Can I get some soup?'

Sam smiles, happy that Ophelia seems stronger, better now. He runs off to the campfire and comes back with a steaming bowl. He sits with her, watching her as she eats. Suddenly, she stops eating and looks up into Sam's eyes. For some reason, she has woken up with a clarity, with a certainty, and with a calm confidence she did not have before. She now knows two things. The first is that Sam is the one. He will be her husband, her protector and her lover for the rest of their live, and secondly, it is time to bury her father.

'Sam, we have to go and bury dad now. It's the right time.' she says.

'Are you sure? It's only been a few hours. Maybe we should wait and go tomorrow.'

'No Sam, it will be okay, I know it will. Dad is at peace now, but he needs a burial – please let's go and do it now.'

'Okay, Oph'. If that's what you want, no problem. I'll go and get some people together.'

Sam gets up to leave, but Ophelia rests her hand on his arm, he sits back down. She gently kisses him on the cheek and smiles. Surprised, he turns his head towards her and she kisses him on the lips. It is the first time. Smiling, he rises and leave the tent, after another, longer, kiss.

As they approach the clearing Sam sends two

of the younger lads to scout ahead, and to keep a lookout. The clearing seems peaceful and restful now. Even Sam can sense something. A change of atmosphere? He does not know what it is, but he is pleased that Ophelia seems to be coping very well, and is now supporting her mother.

They have brought shovels, and four men begin to dig the hole. The group watch silently as Celmar's final resting place becomes deeper. When Sam considers the depth is right, they gather around the hole and gently and reverently lower the body into the hole. To Ophelia, the crumpled body seems smaller. It is as if part of him is no longer there, as if his soul is now missing. It has gone to a better place.

Ophelia has a tear in her eye as she squeezes her mother's shoulder, but she is okay. Sad, but now in control of herself.

They have no preacher, but Sam's father, Raymond stands beside the grave and opens the bible he brought from the village when he left. He has become de facto village captain now. He is a soldier and a fisherman, but also a good speaker, but he keeps it short. The open forest is still not a safe place.

When the assembly leaves the clearing there is little evidence they were there except for the small raised area in one corner with a wooden cross at one end. Celmar's eternal resting place is in the body of the forest with all the plants and animals he knew so well, but it is close to his village, to his family. He would be happy with that.

When the group return to their base by the river they are surprised. There are three armed men waiting for them. Sam has only seen automatic rifles in movies, but these three men had one each. Sams initial fears were dispelled. They are Philipppino, and they are smiling. Two of the village elders were sick and did not go to the burial. They'd told the three what had happened and where everyone was.

Sam's father, Raymond, comes forward and offers his hand to the first man who accepts it and shakes it firmly, then suddenly steps back and smartly salutes.

'Sorry, sir. I didn't recognize your uniform.'

'It's okay sergeant, it's getting a bit worn, and I can't get a new one right now. At ease.'

Raymond raises his eyebrows,

'How did you know I used to be a sergeant,' the surprised man asks.

'Not 'used to be', sergeant, you ARE a serving officer in the Philippine Army. Before Manila fell, the President issued a decree that all retired officers and men are called back into service for the duration of the emergency.'

The leader of the three is John, John Ramos. He is an officer with the Philippine Army. All the armed forces have left their barracks and relocated in the jungle in the hope of forming resistance groups, and protecting their citizens wherever they could.

'Are you Raymond Requilme?' John enquired.

'The sergeant is taken aback that they know his name.

'Yes, I am, how do you know my name?'

'Other villages have told us of an ex-army serviceman holed up in the Jungle. We came to find you. We're establishing a base in the mountains close to Cebu. The area is very high up, so it's easier to defend, and the dense jungle canopy provides cover from the air. If we're careful they won't find us.'

'Sir, I appreciate you looking for me, and I'm so glad the resistance has started, but I can't leave these people. They need me. I am their village captain now.'

'Don't worry sergeant, we are not just a military camp. We have established a settlement for civilians there – it's the size of a small town now. Your people will be welcome, and safe there, we'll take you back there. You will all be better protected, and among friends, Food is not plentiful, but I expect they'll eat better than they do now. We get regular food drops from the Americans.'

Raymond smiles.

'Well, sir that's all very good news. Do you want to stay the night and leave in the morning?'

The lieutenant shakes his head.

'We have to move at night. The Japs normally sleep at night, and we're good at keeping quiet. We should be able to reach Osamis in a few hours. Once we get there, we have some transport trucks. We're getting better organized. We've carried out a few raids and hit their supply routes, but we don't do it close to our base, to put them off the scent. Can you ask your people to rest for a few hours? We will leave at dusk.'

◆ ◆ ◆

Akime's encampment is quiet. Some of his men are uncomfortable at killing civilians on the slightest pretext, but they could not say anything. Akime is volatile and unpredictable, to go against him might cost you your life.

The men ate food in a sombre mood. The bland an badly cooked taste reminded them of the good food they'd had the night before, and the man they had killed. Akime misread the mood.

'Don't worry lads, we'll go after another village tomorrow. There's lots more of them to kill. We've only just started.'

His men have trouble sleeping in the intense heat. The only fan is in Akime's tent, and it doesn't do much to reduce the heat and humidity. Although it is a little easier at night.

Klaus is detailed to guard the food supplies, so he sleeps on his own in the tent with the supplies. It is gone midnight when he dozes off.

The darkest, quietest time is around three a.m. Most birds and animals are then quiet and asleep, but the Santilmo does not sleep. The wisps of smoke gently rising from the ground are accompanied by a crackling sound which becomes louder as the smoke swirls and forms into a shape. The noise is getting louder and Klaus is awakened by it, and by the sight and the smell of his visitor. Only he can hear see and smell to monster, to all around the tent, everything is quiet.

The terrified man stares up as the apparition looms over him with it's open, endless black mouth and it's accusing eyes. One ghostly hand reaches over and picks up a turnip. It's hand hovers in the air for a few seconds holding the large vegetable above the frightened man.

'No, please, don't hurt me. I only...'

No more sound escapes his mouth as the arm of the Santilmo descends, pushing the hard vegetable into Klaus' mouth. It is too big for his mouth, and as his lips stretch wide his lower jaw is forced out of it's socket and broken. His elongated face is contorted in agony as the Santilmo pushes the turnit even further in until it blocks the oesophagus and the windpipe. Starved of air, the desperate man's face turns blue as he struggles to get air into his lungs.

The agony lasts for just a few minutes, until the life leaves his body. The apparition above him seems to smile a ghoulish smile, just slightly, as the man takes his last breath.

Akime finds his body in the morning when he marches into the tent to scream at the lad for being late, and finds his contorted corpse with its misshapen head. The official story is that the hungry lad tried to eat the vegetable and choked on it. Akime knows that is not what really happened.

Trekking through the tropical Philippine jungle at night can be scary, and dangerous, but natives of the forest are more at home than those who've never seen or been in a jungle before. This helps the jungle villagers, and the undercover resistance fighters keen to take advantage of all their enemy's weaknesses.

After travelling for nearly five hours they reach a dry and dusty road.

'They can sit here and wait for a while until the truck comes, just keep off the road and in the bush. The first truck will have a Japanese flag, and two guys in Japanese uniforms. Don't worry. They're our guys. We have a few men and girls who speak Japanese, and we've managed to capture some uniforms – we can usually get by. In the towns the enemy troops are very efficient, but in the jungle they are quite haphazard, and easy to fool.'

It does not take long before the low rumble of a motor wakes those that had managed to doze off. The lieutenant strides into the road as the two trucks approach. The driver and his partner dismount and help the villagers into the truck behind.

Day is breaking as the two trucks start their rise into Mount Labalasan, the tallest mountain is Cebu. The temperature starts to drop as the light breaks over distant peaks. The cooler temperature means the area is good for growing vegetables, and the rugged terrain, with outcrops, and unclimbable peaks with deep valleys means it is difficult for the invaders to reach. Up untill now, no Japanese units have made it very far from the base, but now, well established lookouts and armed groups of resistance fighters means that, if they do try to come, the locals are well prepared. Dense coverings provide a 100% tree canopy which totally covers any activity beneath, so air attacks and landings are not an option.

It was from here that the Southern Resistance movement was formed and continues to grow.

The rickety army truck reaches a small clearing and turning area and the soldiers dismount.

'This is as far as the truck goes, I'm afraid. You'll have a three hour uphill trek until you meet our lowest outpost, they'll look after you from there. I'll be with you some of the way, so you won't get lost, and I've brought plenty of water. I know there are some sick and elderly here, so you can take it slowly, you don't have to hurry, no-one is chasing you.'

It is tough going, and, with rests, they meet up with lookouts after four hours. The sun is rising high in the sky now, and, the lookouts help the group up the steep final distance, hauling them over precipices with ropes and carrying the weak on stretchers when needed.

Finally, dense jungle gives way to a large clearing. Large and small huts are lined up in organized rows, all with green leafy roofs so as to be invisible from the air. A short woman of about fifty years comes forward as the group enter the clearing.

Welcome. I'm Marjorie. I hope your journey wasn't too bad. We have a large hut for you. It's a bit tight, but it's clean. I think you'll be comfortable.

As the group began to wander off, Lieutenant John catches Raymond's eye and takes him to one side.

'Once you've got your group settled in, please come and find me over there at the barracks. We are planning some activities and I need to discuss them with you. You are a great asset. We have about fifty enlisted men here, but only a couple of officers and a few sergeants. Come and find me in an hour or two.'

Raymond feels good. They have a 'barracks'. It feels like they really are beginning to fight back now. He goes to the hut assigned to the villagers He finds them busy settling in and in good spirits. He seeks out his son.

'Sam, I have to go to the army barracks. They want me to get involved in their operations here. I'll need you to keep things in order here with the villagers,'

Sam looks at his father quizzically.

'Dad, I don't want to stay here as a babysitter, I want to be working with you and the other men fighting the Japanese.' he looks hurt.

'Son, we've got more than fifty experienced soldiers here. Let me get to know what's happening first. I'll have a word with the lieutenant later, see if we can bring you in, but you don't have any military experience, and we can't train you at this time. Let me see what I can do.' He puts an arm on his sons shoulder.

'Okay, dad, I understand. But, please try – I'm fit and capable – you know I am.' his father nods as he walks away.

In the 'barracks' Lieutenant Ramos sees Raymond approaching and meets him at the door.

'Come on in. You've joined us at a good time. There's an operation tonight. I know you've had a hard couple of days, but are you up for it?'

'I'm more than ready, sir. It's time we started on the offensive.'

'Glad you feel that way, sergeant. I especially wanted you to be part of this, that's why we came looking for you. It's going to happen in the area that you live – so you should know the territory. You'll have a band of twelve men. They're all enlisted men, I'll bring them in shortly so you can get to know them, but let me explain first, then we'll get your men in here and you can brief them yourself.

The mood in Akime's makeshift camp is sombre. They have just buried Fritz. His body was wrapped from head to toe before he was put in the ground. Nobody wants to look at his distorted and disfigured head, and the wide-eyed look of terror still on his face.

The quiet is shattered when the radio comes alive with a shrill 'brrrrr'. Akime is closest and answers within seconds. He speaks with his local commander for a few minutes then finishes the call.

'Right, men. Gather round. We have new orders. Supplies are running low for our troops in Cebu. Our engineers have repaired the rail line into the city. The bridge at Sangat in San Fernando was damaged, but our engineer say it will support a train now. Our orders are to join the train at Sangat and accompany it through to Cebu – they think there may be insurgents along the way, and want it protected through to Cebu. We can use the horse and cart to get us there, but it will still take several hours, so we need to pack up now. The train is due at Sangat at eleven p.m. We should be there by ten p.m. to check the area out.'

They pack up the cart with the left-over food and supplies and are on their way by late afternoon.

***

Raymond stands before a rudimentary chalk board in the only private room in the barracks. Twelve eager, and younger man wait for him to start. It is three years since sergeant Requilme has been in charge of men, but it seems like yesterday. He is happy to be back in his element. He draws lines on the board.

'We've had news that the Japs are re-opening the railway from Mactan through to Cebu. They desperately need it open to bring supplies through for their troops. The bridge at Mactan was damaged during the invasion, not by us, but by the Japs, but now they need it. Our informants tell us that it is repaired, and they plan to bring the first shipment through tonight.' A lad at the back of the room raises his hand.

'Are we to take the train, sir? Won't we need more men?'

'If we were going to take the train we would need more men, but that is not the plan. The enemy think they're safe because there are few of us, and we don't have many resources, but we have a surprise for them.' The sergeant looks around smiling as his men look at each other wondering what he could mean. In the corner of the room there are three boxes covered by a sheet, no-one has paid them any attention. The sergeant walks over and theatrically pulls the sheet off. There are gasps form the assembled men as three wooden crates are exposed all with 'DYNAMITE – HANDLE WITH CARE' stencilled on them.

'Are they for real, sir?'

'Yes, they're real alright – courtesy of our American friends. They may have left the islands, but they have not abandoned us. We're in contact with them daily and they send in food and medical supplies – and sometimes, special consignments like this. They sent these boxes in especially for this job. We're working on weakening the Japanese forces ready for the Americans to come back in. General

MacArthur has promised us he will be back, and I believe him. Come on, we need to get going, I want to be there by dusk to scout the area – we're not sure what resistance we'll meet. Only pack what you will need. The truck can only take us to a spot two miles from the railway station – we'll have to carry the stuff on foot the rest of the way.'

Their spirits are high as the young soldiers set about packing the truck and preparing for the journey. As well as the explosives there are hand grenades and a rocket launcher. They are better supplied now than they were before the war.

Before they leave there is something the sergeant has to do.

'Son, can I have a word with you?' Raymond calls Sam away from his work, chopping a big pile of logs for firewood.'

'Sure, Dad, what is it?'

'I've got a mission tonight, son. I'm leading men to blow up the bridge between Mactan and Cebu. You can't tell anyone, it must be secret, okay. I just wanted to tell you because if anything goes wrong you need to look after the villagers.' He sees the look of dismay on his son's face.

'Don't worry, son. We'll be fine. We don't expect to directly engage with the enemy, and we're well armed. I also wanted to tell you that the lieutenant has agreed for you to join the troops here, as a recruit. You'll have to train with us and act as support for a few months before you can come out on missions with us. Is that okay?' The boy's face brightens.

'Thanks, dad, that's great. I really appreciate it. While we're talking, there's something I want to ask you. I'm planning to ask Ophelia to marry me. Is that okay with you.'

Raymond smiles broadly as he shakes Sam's hand.

'It's about time, son. You two act as if you are married already. I'm very pleased for you.' The two men embrace. It's time for the sergeant to go.

In the middle of the village, the old army truck stands ready, with the armaments safely packed at the front, the men squeezed in behind. Sergeant Requilme climbs up beside the driver and they slowly trundle out of the village.

The hike through the forest carrying their equipment is arduous, especially for the young men who have seen little action before. The sergeant is pleased that he has carried a box of grenades for two mile and is hardly panting, while around him, much younger men are sweating and struggling.

They finally come to a stop on the top of a hill. Below is the wide river, with the railway bridge spanning the two sides. Raymond lifts his binoculars and scans the area. There is no visible activity. He looks at his watch – they have four or five hours before the train comes through and there is much to do. When they reach the bridge, Requilme sends a man to scout the area. He crosses the bridge very carefully, but there is no activity anywhere. He checks the buildings and the loading platform on the far side of the bridge and reports back to the sergeant.

Raymond listens carefully to the report and makes his decision.

'We'll set the charges this side. We have cover in the trees and bushes, and if we get it right, we can blow the bridge while the train is on it, so they will lose it all.'

American engineers have sent them clear instructions as to where they should put the explosives, and how much they should use. They do not have timers, so they have to wait and set off the explosion at the best time by hand.

Working with their shirts off in the fierce afternoon heat, the men tie the bundle to the bridge supports and run the wires along the struts to a control box about a hundred meters away in the forest. They have just finished their work when a lookout calls them on the radio. Raymond nods and turns to his men.

'Watch out lads, be careful now – there's some activity on the other side of the bridge by the boarding platform.'

CHAPTER 10.

NO MORE SUPPLIES

Akime and his men reach the old train platform with time to spare. It is deserted. Weeds have begun to grow through the cracks in the pavements and on the railway tracks. There is evidence of the repairs the engineers have made – Akime can see where new sections of track have been welded, and fresh support posts put underneath. He is happy that he will soon be back in Cebu, at least part way to civilization. If they had been keen, they could have seen through binoculars, men scrabbling along the bridge supports on the other side of the bridge and disappearing into the jungle, but they were not looking. Akime talks with someone over the radio then reports back to his men.

'The train is on time, lads. Let's get everything onto the platform ready, so we can load it quickly when the train arrives. We want to be away from here as soon as possible.'

From their vantage point across the valley, Raymond watches the industrious Japanese soldiers pile boxes of vegetables and other stuff close to the edge of the platform and settle down for the wait. The sergeant realises that his men can relax too.

'It won't be here for a couple of hours yet, you can take a rest. We'll know it's coming about thirty minutes before it gets here. It's a steam train – we'll see the flume of steam rising into the air from at least two or three miles away, and it is obviously going to stop on the other side of the bridge to pick up those supplies before it comes over.'

His men relax and settle down, grateful for the breather. All is quiet for a few hours until a lookout shakes the sergeant's shoulder.

'It's coming, sir. Look, you can just see those wisps of steam rising out of the jungle. Raymond shakes his head vigorously, it's time for action.

Akime and his men have also spotted the steam from the approaching train, and rouse themselves in readiness.

After twenty minutes, the lumbering black engine pulls up alongside the platform. There are five carriages behind, heavily laden with supplies of all sorts. In the front engine there are four men, the driver and his assistant and two soldiers. They jump down off the train as it pulls up.

'We're looking for sergeant Akime.'

'That's me,' shouts Akime as he approaches from the other end.

'Sir,' the two jump to attention. 'We have orders to hand over to you here. We'll ride with you to Cebu, but you're in charge now.' They salute and jump back on the train.

In ten minutes, all the boxes are neatly stacked in the second carriage and the men all jump into the engine compartment.

'Hang on, men. We have to guard this train. I want three men stationed in the middle of the train and three men at the back. We know there's resistance fighters around here. Stay alert, and report to me if you see any activity.' The appointed men alight and move to the other parts of the train, leaving Akime and the other two men in the front with the drivers. They set off.

Sergeant Requilme is watching closely as the train crosses the bridge. It is longer than the bridge, so the final carriage is still leaving the far bank as the front engine reaches the other end. He joins the two men guarding the detonator.

'Now's the time men, do it now.'

Both men have their hands on the plunger and push it sharply down. It takes about three seconds for the activation, then they see the first flash before they hear the sound. Four flashes follow quickly as the ear-splitting booms reach the fighters in the hillside. The train is halfway over the bridge, but slides backwards as the bridge falls away from under it and the last carriages pull it backwards.

Akime sees the flashes and watches the final carriage start to fall as he hears the bang. He feels the engine being pulled backwards, and thinks quickly.

'Jump men. Quickly, jump.' He pushes one of his men off the train and follows him, with his other man following quickly. They make a soft landing in the dense ferns, and watch as the engine behind them is dragged into the ravine below, with the driver and his mate screaming, arms flailing, as they plummet to their deaths. Three hundred yards away, just below the bridge, Raymond and his men are dancing and congratulating each other.

'Careful men, we mustn't make a noise – there could still be Japanese troops around – we can't be too careful.'

Indeed, there are enemy troops close by, but they have other things to worry about than chasing local resistance fighters.

Akime knows they are close to Cebu now – maybe eight hours on foot, and they have no radio.

'Come on. We'll set off towards Cebu and see if we can find some transport on the way, and a radio. We have to let our command know what has happened, but we must be careful. There are only three of us and we just have our pistols.' Sergeant Akime is fearful he will be blamed. – he should have scouted the area properly; he checked the time – it was eleven p.m.

'Let's get a move on. If we keep going, we can get back by early morning.'

Fritz and Lucas look at each other – they travelled all day and have not slept, but they can see that their sergeant is in no mood to be argued with.

Sergeant Requilme and his jubilant band set off for home. If they'd known that three lone Japanese troops were close by, and poorly armed, they would have taken the time to 'deal' with them, but they did not.

They made good time through the jungle and met up with the truck at the appointed place. They didn't realise it, but the three Japanese were only five minutes behind them. The enemy heard the engine noise as it sped off towards the rebel camp and ran forward hoping to capture it, but as they reached the road the truck was a speck of dust in the distance.

◆ ◆ ◆

After a couple more hours Fritz and Lucas are hungry and exhausted. They have to say something.

'Sergeant, can't we just stop for a while and make some food, and tea. We're exhausted.'

They expected a sharp negative response, but Akime is also tired and needs food.

'Okay, we'll make a campfire and have a short

rest, no more than sixty minutes. Fritz, go and find some dry wood for the fire.'

As Fritz wanders off into the forest, Lucas and Akime set about clearing the area and digging a shallow pit for the fire.

Lucas is the first to hear it. He stops what he is doing and listens. There it is again, a strange crackling and rustling. Hidden from the Japanese pair in a hollow not far away, something was stirring. It was nighttime, but an eerie glow emanated from the hollow.

Mist and sparks slowly rose until the shape forms. The spectral eyes cast around, then it sets off slowly slithering in the direction of the two men. As it navigates the tree and bushes it slowly changes it's form until it was a giant and ghostly snake, making it's way through the forest, but it is not like any normal snake. It has an open mouth with a deep hole which is black inside, and It's eyes are blood red and dead. It is more like a snake with the head of a monster, but it's size has grown. It is far bigger than any natural snake. It is ten metres long from head to the tip of it's tail – the same length as the rope the men had used to hang Celmar.

As it nears Akime, it slows and becomes quieter, but the sergeant hears it and is now on his guard.

He sees it first. Lucas has his back to the tree, and stares at the wild-eyed Akime, wondering why he is acting so strangely. Out of his sight, the monster slithers out onto a branch five metres above the grounds and slowly drops it's tail alongside the tree trunk until it is just inches away from Lucas, who is still staring at his boss whose eyes are transfixed on the ghoulish scene in front of him.

Lucas then senses the presence, hears the crackling and smells the awful stink. By now it is too late. The thing is about three inches thick at the point it curls around his chin and behind his neck. As it tightens, his arms fly up to try to pull it away, but the grip is like iron, slowly gripping and encircling the man's head until it can easily lift the terrified man off the ground.

Akime watches, helpless, as his comrade rises from the ground, gurgling and flailing, his face forced to one side, his eyes and veins bulging, and his breathing coming in shorter and shorter gasps. Akime is unable to move. The macabre scene in front of him reminds him of what they did to Celmar. Lucas loses control of his bowels and small brown streaks appear out of the bottom of his trousers and drips onto the dusty ground below.

After many moments of flailing around, Lucas draws his last breath and hangs there, like a rag doll until the monster is satisfied, then suddenly, the vision is gone. The body of the soldier falls to the ground and all is quiet. Akime still cannot move. He stands there staring down at his fallen comrade, still terrified and frightened to approach. It is at this moment that he realizes that the two of his men who had just died in unworldly circumstances had been two of the men who he'd detailed to hang the old man. Could it be a coincidence?

Fritz returns with an armful of wood to find his comrade on the floor, red-faced, and with his purple tongue hanging out, dead. The man's eyes stare upwards towards and unseen horror. The sergeant sits ten feet away, sobbing uncontrollably, his hands scratching at the ground. He drops the wood and runs over to Akime.

'Sir, sir. What's happened – are you okay?' He pulls the trembling man to his feet, and holds him to prevent him falling again. As the shaking man realizes Fritz is there, he begins to regain his composure.

'What happened here, sir? Who killed Lucas?'

Akime was slowly regaining his senses now.

'It was a snake, son. Bigger than I've ever seen. There was nothing I could do. I tried to free him, but the snake lifted him off his feet. ' The sergeant sways uncertainly, and Fritz lowers him to the ground, so he didn't fall over.

Fritz lights the fire to make some sweet tea – it may help the sergeant. Also, the fire may keep away any more monstrous animals that may be out there, Fritz really hates this place. As he waits for the water to boil, he stares at the lifeless body of his friend. They can't bury him, they have no tools. His sergeant twists and turns, and moans, sometimes coherent, sometimes not. He thinks of leaving Akime and trying to get back to the city on his own, but if Akime ever made his way back and told the story, he would be executed. He boils the water as quickly as he can – he wants to be on his way out of this deadly place.

He gives the sergeant the sweetened tea and after a few moments the man calms down, then falls into a sleep, Fritz waits. Although exhausted, he cannot sleep. In a few hours it will be dawn, his sergeant would wake up and they'd continue through the forest, it would no longer be dark, any unspeakable horrors will go away until the next night.

◆ ◆ ◆

News of the bridge bombing, and the train crash reach the camp before Sergeant Aquilme and his colleagues arrive back at the rebel base. As they roll into camp they are greeted with hugs and smiles – no-one shouted. They know better than to make loud noises – you can never be too sure.

Raymond was welcomed back into the villagers hut as a hero, which he was. He hugs Sam, who cannot hold back a tear.

'I'm proud of you, Dad.' He hugs his father and does not let him go.

◆ ◆ ◆

Fritz and the sergeant make it into the camp mid-morning on the following day. By then, everyone knows of the disastrous event of the previous night. Other soldiers run to assist them as the bedraggled men stagger along the approach road. The commanding officer is in a meeting with his senior officers when he hears the news that these two, the only survivors, have arrived back at the camp.

'I want to see them, now. Bring them up here. We'll continue this meeting later.'

The two bedraggled soldiers shuffle into the room, Fritz let go of the sergeant for a moment to salute the senior officer, but quickly grabs Akime's should before he falls over.

'What's the matter with him?' The captain addresses his comments at Fritz.

'Sir, he had an… 'experience' in the jungle. I left

the camp to get firewood, and when I got back I found him like this, and private Lucas was dead on the ground.'

'Akime stared silently at the wall. He does not acknowledge his commander. He seems in a trance.'

Sit him in a chair, man, before he falls over.' The captain gestures to an armchair in the corner. Fritz guided him into the comfortable chair and resumed his position, at attention, before his commander, who now addresses him directly.

'What the hell happened, son. You had a battle-seasoned group of ten soldiers – how could you let this happen. Did you check out the area when you arrived? How could you let these savages blow up the train under your noses, if you'd even just checked the bridge you would have found the explosives, or maybe even have confronted the saboteurs.

'Sir, when we arrived at the railway tracks we just stayed there waiting for the train – The sergeant told us just to rest and wait there.' The captain snorted.

'Was Akime okay then? Or was he like this?'

'No sir, he was fine at this time. No sign of any problems – he was just tired, but he seemed okay. I think something happened to the sergeant after the explosion – when we were in the forest. There was something strange about how Lucas died, sir.'

'What do you mean, son.'

'Well sir, I've never seen a man killed that way by a snake, he was strangled. Two men should easily be able to fight off a snake. It didn't bite him, it strangled him. I can't see why he couldn't fight it off, especially with the sergeant to help, and the sergeant seemed in fear of his life when I got back, like he'd seen a ghost, and that the ghost was still with him.'

They both stare at the feeble bumbling man in the corner.

'Get him out of here, son. Get him to the infirmary. I have never seen anything like this before. Let's see if they can do anything for him. We can't afford to lose any soldier right now. That's all for now.'

Fritz salutes, and helps Akime to stand and limp to the door. The commander closes the door behind the departing men.

Japan has been making a passable 'scotch' whisky for many years now, but connoisseurs still preferred single malts which came from the highlands – Captain Yamoyo is partial to Genmorangie, and had crates of it sent to him from the mainland, at least he did until deliveries from the Japanese mainland virtually ceased nearly three months; he is down to his last two bottles. Nevertheless, he opens the bottom drawer of his desk and pours a generous glass; his second today and downs it in a couple of gulps.

Things are getting out of control here. He puts his glass down and tries to call his commander for the third time that day. This time he got through. After waiting many more minutes he is finally put through to General Yamashita. The commander of all the Japanese forces in the Philippines.

'General Yamashita, it's Yamoto here, sir. I have bad news. The train which was supposed to come yesterday to relieve our food shortage yesterday did not arrive. Rebels blew up the rail line again – they destroyed the bridge at Mactan again. Completely this time, and the whole train with it. So we lost the train, the supplies, and the supply route. We had troops in the area who should have checked the bridge, but they did not. Most of them lost their lives, but I'm looking to discipline those that are left.'

He had no intention of telling his boss that the sergeant in charge of the operation had returned to the camp as a gibbering idiot.

'That's not good news, son. We were all relying on that train route to keep you going. I'm not sure what you can do now. Give me some time and I'll get back to you.' The general never did call back.

Over the following months. The captain tries to feed his troops, but every time he sends them out looking for food, fewer of them come back. The rebels are growing stronger and more confident, he'd has to put his men on half rations.

There are rumours that the Americans are coming back now. The commander knows that if the Yanks return in numbers, it will be the end for the Japaneses occupation. After all the atrocities and murders his troops have committed, he does not imagine they will be treated well if they are captured. It is time to speak to General Yamashita again.

'Sir, we are desperate now. Can you send supplies by helicopter and drop them for us? We can't hold out much longer.' There was silence at the other end for a few seconds, the captain took the time to pour himself another whisky. Eventually, Yamashita sighs.

'Son, I've been told by our command in Tokyo that we're on our own. No more support, no more supplies. They know we are on the ropes now, they've seen us failing. They've seen the Philippine rebels getting stronger and they are abandoning us now that the rebels have American support, and the U.S. troops are on their way back here.'

'I see, sir. What are we to do?

'My advice is to try to get back to Japan while you still can. If there are any boats still in the port, take them – try to get into international waters, try to get back to Japan if you can. I'm sorry, son, we're all on our own now. Good luck.' The line goes dead.

The captain decides to reflect on their position and make up his mind what to do in the morning.

The loss of the freight train, and more and bolder attacks by the local rebels have two big consequences for the invaders. They are experiencing a lot more losses and set-backs than they anticipated. The city is dependent on food being brought in from the outlying villages, or from other cities. There was little food coming from the close by villages now as their inhabitants had all fled into the mountains to escape the Japanese soldiers, and their train supply routes and most road supplies had now been destroyed The local population are growing in their aggression, his the troops have barely enough food. Morale is not good.

Akime was diagnosed with PTSD and has now been hospitalized. The medics could not get anything out of him except 'Ghostly snake… awful stench… piercing eyes'.

He slept most of the time, but after a while he was deemed fit for release, but only for desk duties. He'd only had one visitor during his time in the hospital – Fritz had been loyal to him, and now came to help him back to barracks. He smiles as he enters the ward.

'How are you feeling today, boss? Today's the day – I've come to help you back to the barracks.' The sergeant that left the hospital leaning on Fritz' arm is a hollow version of his former aggressive self. There is no fight, no strength, no anger. All that has been replaced by a deep fear, a despair, and a growing belief that the evil events had been caused by his deeds and the murder committed by the four of them that afternoon so long ago.

The damaged sergeant would not see action again in this war, or any other. Fritz is detailed to look after him, basically to nurse him, and keep him out of the way. The commander of the Japanese troops in Cebu, is facing difficulties. The rebels are getting stronger everywhere, supported by the Americans who, according to all accounts, are planning a re-invasion – they will support the Philippine forces in pursuing the dejected and diminished Japanese

Fritz is in a good mood today. The men were are going home. They were told it was 'a strategic retreat to prepare for the re-invasion'. None of the men believe that. They know they are beaten and need to get home before they are captured.

◆ ◆ ◆

The mood in the rebel camp in the mountains is good. Their fighting forces have grown to more than five hundred men. Raymond Requilme is now a captain, and Sam has replaced him as a sergeant. The villages around are being left alone now – the Japanese soldiers have their own problems, and most of them have retreated to the safety of Cebu city.

Over the intervening months the camp soldiers have built an airstrip. American engineers dropped plans with their regular supplies. It was completed a week ago and they are expecting the first troop carrying plane to arrive today.

'This is so exciting! Come and see.' Ophelia pulled sam into the mess hall. There are seating and cooking facilities for three hundred people, which is just as well because they are expecting more than two hundred American troops to arrive on the plane at around ten a.m.

The welcoming party includes Raymond and Sam, as well as other local leaders. They assemble on the landing strip when they hear the engines and see the large troop carrier appear above them. The lads light beacons at each end of the airstrip to guide the welcome visitors down. It takes maybe five minutes for the large plane to circle and make its approach, but it is not long before the large double doors at the front of the plane open, and smiling American troops begin to make their way down the stairway onto the Philippine soil that they had left not so long ago. Lieutenant Ramos steps forward and salutes the young captain who is the first to descend.

'Welcome back, sir. I'm Lieutenant John Ramos. We're pleased to see you guys.' Captain Lindsey Gordon smartly returns the salute. As more and more servicemen begin to pour out of the belly of the plane and unload their supplies, Ramos leads the party towards the mess tent, a hot meal awaits the welcome foreigners after their long journey.

'It's been a long struggle captain, we're so glad you're back.' Ophelia and Sam sit next to the senior officers at the head of the table.

'We're glad to be back ma'am. The battle's nearly over now, but we know that there's still a lot of work to do.' says the young officer.

'Well, now you guys are here, I'm sure it will speed things up.'

'I'm so glad of that, sir. Ophelia and I are waiting for everything to be over so we can get married.' says Sam.

Captain Gordon looks at Sam and Ophelia.

'Why wait? We have an army chaplain with us. He can marry you if you want.'

The two lovers look at each other. Ophelia is the first to speak.

'Yes. Oh, yes please. That would be wonderful. Can you excuse me please?' With a tear of joy in her eye, Ophelia goes off to tell her mother.

'That's wonderful, sweetheart. I only wish your father were here to see it.' Ophelia nods quietly.

'He will be, mum, he will be.' She forces a smile and hugs her mother again before rushing back to join Sam who is discussing the details with the captain.

'It doesn't need to be a grand affair, a simple ceremony will do. We have many other things we have to concentrate on.' Sam said. The captain nods in agreement.

'Yes, I agree, but it'll be a great thing to do. It will lift everyone's spirits. How long do you need to prepare?' By now Ophelia has joined them again and joins the conversation.

'How about a week, captain. I already have a wedding dress. My mother's been working on it since Sam and I got engaged.' she beams.

'Well that's settled then. You guys set everything up. I'll talk to the chaplain and make sure everything is in order.'

CHAPTER 11.

THE WEDDING AND
THE DEATH.

By the end of the meal, everyone in the camp knows that Sam and Ophelia are soon to be married.

Sergeant Ramos agrees to give the girl away and the whole camp works towards the ceremony, and the party afterwards. The Americans have brought plentiful supplies of food with them. This will be a great day. The start of a new life, not just for Sam and Ophelia, but for everyone in the camp. They feel secure now. The japs are fleeing their posts throughout the Philippines. Locals have taken back the radio stations and they're getting real news now. Most of the invaders have abandoned their posts and are fleeing, trying to get back to their homeland by air or sea, any means they can find. The command in Tokyo have abandoned them – they have their own problems and will soon surrender to the Americans.

'Do you remember this, sweetheart?' Maria, Ophelia's mum, is holding up the faded yellow dress that Ophelia wore on her birthday, nearly a year ago. Ophelia laughed.

'Of course I do. That was my favourite dress, until now.' Ophelia looked down at the bright white wedding gown. Her mother is now busy with pins, making the final adjustments. The day after tomorrow will be her wedding day, She will become Mrs. Ophelia Requilme. Her heart is bursting, the only thing missing is her father. That was a thought she needs to put to the back of her mind, at least for now.

The next forty eight hours go by very quickly, and Ophelia soon finds herself walking down the makeshift aisle towards the chaplain, an older, kindly man, who stood waiting under the large cross hastily erected by the fresh American troops and their Philippine helpers.

◆ ◆ ◆

Across the mountains in Cebu, the Japanese troops are preparing to depart. Akime and Fritz will leave on the last, large troop ship. Akime has hardly worked in the months he has been back. Fritz has almost become his full-time helper.

Another sergeant comes into the barracks to check all is ready. Everyone is busy packing their things ready for the journey, except for Akime, who still just sits there staring into space with Fritz by his side.

'If you two have nothing to do, take a final walk into the forest – see if you can find some fruit or vegetables or something for the journey. Hurry up. We'll be leaving soon.'

The two set off with bags, in the hope of finding something they can eat. About fifteen minutes into the forest they find a mango tree. The fruits are green, not ripe yet, but they can be eaten, with salt. Akime is no help at all. He just sits there while Fritz climbs the tree.

For a few moments, the two do not notice the faint wisps of smoke at the base of the tree. It is Akime who first hears the faint crackling, and smells the awful stench that he has now come to dread. In a brief moment of clarity he shouts up to his comrade.

'Fritz, get down here. It's coming.' Akime screams hysterically.

By this time Fritz is high up in the tree, getting the final fruits. Below him he can see the ball of mist, but he can't hear the noise, or smell the stench.

Akime watches, mouth agape and unable to speak now, as the beast forms, it's endless black mouth open wide and its sinister beady eyes fixed on the burbling man. As the monster hovers above the ground and moves upwards, Akime detects a faint smile on the monster. In a couple of seconds, the monster is at the top if the tree, next to Fritz who is petrified with fear, and tightly clutching a nearby branch to stop himself from falling. The Santilmo stares at Fritz who can now smell the pungent stench and almost chokes on it. The ghoul glances away to the thick stump of the branch where it joins the tree. It snaps like a twig.

Fritz now feels himself falling and just has time to look down and see the ground coming up to meet him. Akime watches helplessly as Fritz plummets to the ground, his head contacts the earth with a sharp crack before his body follows. His neck is broken completely, leaving his head at an unusual and macabre angle, His lifeless eyes stare directly, and accusingly, at Akime.

The sergeant is still sat on the ground, trembling and staring at the lifeless body when two men appear, They have been sent to find the long overdue pair and are guided to the spot by Akime's incessant wailing. The sergeant has now completely lost his mind. He grips to his rescuers and will not let go.

'It's coming, it's coming. God help me.' These

were the only words the dribbling man could say in his brief moments of lucidity.

Akime cannot know of the celebrations taking place over the mountains. Hundreds of people are laughing and dancing while the tragic scene in the forest unfurls.

◆ ◆ ◆

'I do.' Ophelia smiles as she says the magic words. The chaplain slips the ring on her finger and the young couple kiss.

'I now pronounce you man and wife.' The chaplain ends the ceremony at exactly the same time as Fritz' neck vertebrae are splitting apart and severing his spinal cord in the forest far away.

◆ ◆ ◆

'Poor bastard. In a few days he would have been home.' The two soldiers look down at the still staring Fritz.

'What are we going to do. We have to get back. There's no time to bury him, and we can't take the gibbering idiot back as well as carry the body.' He looks over at Akime who is now staring at a tree and dribbling.

'Come on, we'll tell them we buried him – no-one is ever going to know.' The other man nods, and they set off through the jungle, pulling Akime along with them. Fritz is still staring, lifeless, up at the sky as a vulture descends from the sky and begins its grisly work.

Captain Yamoto looks out over the bay from his office, the former mayoral chamber, as his men board the final boat, which will leave in two hours time. Philippine and American troops are on their way, he has heard that enemy troops are boarding transporters in Manila to come to Cebu and reclaim it for the republic. He looks at his watch. Unless there are last minute problems, the ship will be in international waters and halfway to Japan by the time they reach the city. They only have hours to spare.

Around him, clerks are filling boxes with files and equipment and carrying it away. Yamoto will be glad to get back to his country, to his wife, but he knows he is leaving not as a victor, but as the vanquished. He is worried about his reception when he gets back. He's tried to contact his bosses in the homeland, but there is no reply. The Japanese do not tolerate failure. This is not his failure, but that will not matter. He will be blamed, along with the other 'failing' soldiers.

As he watches, Akime is pushed on board. He is now in a wheelchair – it's easier than assisting him along.

Two days later, Akime is wheeled into the doctors office in Tokyo. The overworked doctor looks up from his paperwork at the shattered soldier. He knows the man's history, that he'd lost his mind after failing to stop the enemy blowing up a train – a turning point in the war.

The young psychiatrist regards the dribbling man with disdain, almost as an enemy. If it had not been for this animal, and other soldiers like him

Japan would have been victorious. Their glorious emperor would not have had to surrender, in utter humiliation, to the Americans. He looks up at an orderly.

'Does he have any next of kin?'

'No sir, he lived with his mum, but she's in a nursing home herself now. She doesn't understand what's happening. He's on his own.' The doctor nods.

'I don't expect any improvement, I don't think he's fit for the general ward. He can't even take a shit without help. Put him in the basement with the other long-term cases. He's not going to get any visitors, so no need to fuss over him too much.'

The 'basement' is more like a jail. There are ten individual rooms. Akime is not considered safe on a ward. He has to be in a single cell. All the rooms are locked with a bucket in the corner as a toilet.

He is wheeled into the farthest cell and without a word, the attendants pull him out and dump him on the thin mattress. They leave without a word.

◆ ◆ ◆

In the Philippines, life is gradually getting back to normal. Remnants of the bedraggled Japanese army still try to get home, stealing fishing boats and sometimes surrendering. Some soldiers hide in the jungle and keep away from people, only to surrender many years later.

The U.S. soldiers are back in full force now, helping the battered islands to rebuild, and enabling America to consolidate their foothold in South East Asia.

None of the villagers want to return to their village. There are too many memories. Sam and his father lead a group of U.S troops and a chaplain to the village. The bones of the dead villagers are scattered everywhere, the forest carnivores feasted well for months and did not care where they left their scraps. Sam and his father gather all the bones they could find together into one pile. They decide to divide all the remains them up between five graves, for the five dead villagers. As long as their relatives have somewhere to come and visit their departed relatives, they will never know.

Many of the shacks are now blown down and derelict. Raymond decides they will burn the remains of the village, to signify a new start and put the past behind them.

Sam is in the military proper now, he will soon sit his promotion exams, and Raymond is again retired, but they all live in military accommodation for families. It is safer and more substantial than anything she'd ever lived in before. Her mother, Maria, lives with them.

After a few months Sam comes home one day to find Ophelia crying, and her mother holding her tightly.

'Whatever is the matter, sweetheart.' Ophelia looks up into his eyes.

'Sweetheart. These are tears of joy. I'm pregnant – we're going to have a baby.' She bursts out crying again. Sam holds his wife tightly, he is so happy. They will be a family soon. His life will be complete.

Maria sets about making baby clothes, and the whole encampment buzzes with excitement. As she got bigger, Ophelia starts planning their future. She has put all thought of study, of becoming a lawyer, behind her, happily. She is content as a wife and mother – she will try to give her child all the things she never had.

In her quieter moments, Ophelia remembers her past life, a life she would never know again. She misses village life, the simplicity, the fun and laughter of the fiestas. But most of all she misses her father. She spoke to him in the stillness of her alone time, asking his opinions, seeking his help with problems. He is still with her, and she feels comfortable with his closeness and protection.

◆ ◆ ◆

Ophelia flinches. The gel is cold. She lifts her head up to watches the doctor slides the ultrasound wand over her now distended tummy. Beside her, Sam sits and smiles. He squeezes her hand as she complains that the gel, and the doctors hands are cold.

'No need to complain, sweetheart, it'll be over soon. How long do we have to go, doctor?'

The young doctor smiles. Originally from West Virginia, she completed her training in Washington before joining up as an army doctor. The Philippines is her first posting, there is a baby boom following the jubilation of the new freedom after the oppressive Japanese occupation. She trained as an obstetrician, but she didn't expect to be so busy.

'I think about two weeks now, Sam. She should take things easy. No strenuous exercise, no long trips, okay?'

Sam and Ophelia both nod. They are still holding hands.

Twelve days later, the couple are back in the hospital. Her waters have broken. It is time. Luckily, the same young doctor is in attendance.

Two nurses bustle round Ophelia, after a couple of hours they give her a face mask.

'Take deep breaths when you feel the pains. It will help. You're fully dilated now. I'm going to get the doctor.'

Ophelia squeezes Sam's hand until it is white. Although it is painful, he will not let go.

From the bottom of the bed the nurses are watching the expectant mother closely.

'It's coming.' The older nurse calmly folds back the sheets and steps back for the doctor to approach. The top of a tiny head is now poking through.

Sam wipes Ophelia's sweaty brow. The girl is red-faced and panting.

'You're doing fine 'Phe. Almost there.'

The delivery took less than thirty minutes and the baby was healthy. The little boy screams as the nurses wrap him.

In faraway Tokyo, life has not changed for Akime for nearly a year. His tortured mind spends every day dreaming of demons, of pain, of misery. His room is rarely cleaned and it stinks. He is taken out about one a week for a shower. His pail is emptied at that time, it has usually overflowed by then. He is emaciated and his body covered with sores. He gets food of some sort most days. Left-over rice with rotten fish, sometimes stale bread; if the jailers have no leftovers from their meal, he gets none. The water he gets is from the well outside, sour, and contaminated by the urine which flows into it, but he drinks it – he has no choice.

He used to read, the guard would sometimes throw a newspaper in, but it has been many months since he bothered.

When he was put in the place he had a uniform, it was crumpled and dirty, but it was recognisable as a sergeant's uniform. At first the jailers called him 'The sarge' mockingly. Over the months it has worn away. For a while he had worn his soiled underpants, but now he is naked, like an animal.

Today is a lucky day for him. The larger jailer has thrown in half a bowl of cold noodles. He takes it to the corner. He feels safe in the corner. In a minute, the bowl is empty.

As he stares at the bowl, wishing he had more, he sees something in the opposite corner, just beside the bars. A wispy haze is forming. He wipes his eyes in case his vision is blurred, but no. it is still there, and growing, and he can now detect a smell, overpowering, even over the smell of his feces. His eyes widen and his mouth falls open now. He starts to shake – he knows what this is. He has been expecting it. The Santilmo rises, and takes it sparling form, with it's eyes even more red and piercing and it's lip's curled in an evil smile.

Akime finds his voice for the first time in many months, but what comes out is just an insane babble.

'Help me. It's coming. I'm sorry, I'm so sorry. Get away, get away.' Akime screams at the top of his voice. His back is against the wall now and the monster is still approaching.

The guards hear his screams.

'That lunatic is at it again.' The man regards his

hand of cards and lays one down on the table.

'Yeah, it would be better for the rambling fool if he were out of it. It's not even like he's a happy fool. He's frightened of his own shadow, and always looks as if he's seen a ghost.'

His friend nods as the crying and pleading continues.

The unholy vision is now in front of the babbling man. Akime watches as it lifts his bowl from the ground. It lifts the bowl up to his lips as if it is going to feed him. As the edges of the bowl touches his lips that he realises the worst. The painful pressure increases as the bowl is pushed further against his face, His mouth is contorted wider and wider until the taught flesh can take no more.

Wide-eyed, his eyes bulge as the bowl splits his mouth at both edges and relentlessly proceeds to split his jaws wide open. Blood pours down his chin and drips onto his chest as he gurgles. The Santilmo pushes on, effortlessly inserting the china bowl further into the gaping, bloody hole that was the man's mouth.

Through excruciating pain, Akime feels the rim reach the back of his throat and hears his jaw crack as it dislocates.

Relentlessly, the monster continues to effortlessly push the bowl through the mess that was Akime's mouth, through the back of the throat and against the spine – then onward. His spine snaps and his head falls to one side, but the Santilmo continues with it's gristly work, pushing the bowl between the vertebrae, first squashing, then severing the spinal column.

In his last few seconds of life, Akime watches the ghoul pull back, admiring its handiwork He sees a smile on its face now and watches it sink into the floor as his mind goes dark.

As the vile Japanese soldier breathes his last breath, Newly born, Celmar Requilme II. takes his first breath. Sam and Ophelia decided on the name days ago. Ophelia squeezes Sams hand tightly again as the nurse brings over the little bundle, now quiet and content in his mother's arms.

She is sure she can see her father's smile on the little boys face as she cradles him. A tear comes to her eye, but she has a feeling inside that now, finally, all is right with the world.

ABOUT THE AUTHOR

Arthur Crandon

Arthur writes thrillers, suspense and intrigue novels mainly set in South-East Asia. He also writes a blog where he comments on Asian politics and social matters - and his own work.

Arthur is a former British lawyer who worked in the UK, Hong Kong and the Philippines specializing in visas and immigration - a great source of inspiration for his stories.

His time as a warden for the British Embassy in Manila also provided insight for his writing.

In between writing and blogging, Arthur is studying for an M. A. in creative writing and plans further study after that. In his spare time he enjoys music (he is a keyboards player) and cooking.

Arthur is married with five children. He and his wife, Lynnie, divide their time between the UK and Asia.

He has been voted No. 1 by Goodreads readers in their poll - 'Little known authors worth reading'.

BOOKS BY THIS AUTHOR

Deadly Election

Buried treasure. A corrupt politician. A man in the wrong place at just the right time…
The Philippines. Former US Marine Paul McCain has traded in his rifle for a camera as a wildlife photographer. When he spies young villagers unearthing lost WWII gold, he happily captures their cries of delight. But their joyous shouts are drowned in a hail of bullets as McCain witnesses their brutal murder by a ruthless presidential candidate.

Desperate for any allies outside the politician's deadly grip, he's willing to do whatever it takes to bring the powerful leader down. But with his quarry poised to win the election, the clock ticks down on his quest for justice. And taking on a man this connected puts the hardened veteran right in the killer's crosshairs…

Can McCain survive long enough to prevent a murderer from ascending to the Philippines' highest office?

Deadly Election is the first book in the engrossing Asian Intrigue thriller series. If you like tenacious heroes, political scandal, and no-holds-barred action, then you'll love Arthur Crandon's fast-paced adventure.

Final Vengeance

His friends are dead. His girlfriend kidnapped. Some have run away or been killed, but this American Marine has other plans.

He is no stranger to the Philippines, but Paul McCain has never before faced the ruthless evil of the Chinese Mafia. After a failed marriage, buying a hotel in Angeles, the Philippines seemed a good idea for the retired marine. It would take him back to a familiar place where he served years earlier. The familiar places, the cheap alcohol, the girls... Maybe he could forget his wife.

When he bought it, Paul did not know that the local mafia boss, Charlie Wong, also wanted the popular western style hotel. People get kidnapped, people get killed, and people run away frightened, but not Paul – he is made of sterner stuff.

There are many retired US servicemen living in Angeles City. Thousands were stationed there years ago, and many stayed on or returned later, in retirement. They rally to the cause when Paul needs their help.

The battles are long, and bloody. The city is turned upside down while the two sides vie for superiority.. The story does not end well for either side. Plot twists and side plots are weaved to great effect – many secrets are not revealed until the end, and some, not even then.

Bloodline Curse

BLOODLINE CURSE brings to life, in vivid horror, a decades old legend.

"The evils of the father shall be visited on the son, and future generations…"

Who could foretell that the deeds of Rajah Tupas, the founder of the Constantino dynasty, would have consequences beyond the grave.

He watched the burning flesh of the young priest fall from the bones, as the young man died in screaming agony.

Births are supposed to be joyous occasions, but not when the 'baby' is a monstrous fiend intent on devouring human flesh.

Could they kill it? Should they kill it? Why was it still alive? and how many more innocents would die a horrifying death?

If it dies, will that be the end?